THE ETIQUETTE OF BURGLARY

and other stories

Pauline McNulty

Published 2016 by Pauline McNulty
©2016 Pauline McNulty
ISBN 978-1-5262-0267-3
Reprinted 2017

Designed by April Sky Design & Colourpoint Creative Limited Newtownards
www.aprilsky.co.uk

Printed by GPS Colour Graphics Ltd, Belfast

For my family, Mike, Matthew, Thomas and Evie.

PREFACE

When one of my sons lent this little book to a friend, it was duly returned with the comment, "You must have had a dreadful childhood!"

As happy endings are not my forte, he had a point, but I hope you enjoy reading these short stories as much as I have enjoyed writing them.

CONTENTS

THE ETIQUETTE OF BURGLARY

Norris, better known as Soupy, was nervously attempting his first burglary. Coming from a long ancestral line in that profession, he felt it incumbent upon himself, at sixteen years old, to at least make a start on his career. And so, he found himself in a tall Victorian house in a quiet cul-de-sac, contemplating an array of silver trophies and ornate silver-framed photographs on the mantelpiece in front of him.

He wondered what the etiquette of burglary was. Should he remove the photographs before stealing the frames, in case they were of sentimental value to their owner, or just take the lot? He felt sick. Carefully he reached up and lifted down one of the framed photographs. It was heavy, and his hands were hot and sweaty.

'This is it' he thought, 'I've got to take something or ....go home.'

But, before he could finish the thought, a voice sounded behind him.

"Well, well, well – and what are you doing here?'

A cold wave of paralysing fear washed through Norris, and he felt sick and dizzy. His fumbling fingers dropped the frame and the glass shattered, shards skittering across the polished wooden floor.

"Please missus, I never done this before....I'm sorry, really I am, this is me first job, I thought there was nobody here". He began to snivel, tears and snot running down his face in equal measure. It didn't occur to him to simply run down the hall and on out the door.

"So what else have you got to say for yourself?" asked the voice, to which Norris replied,

"I think I'm going to be sick!"

"Oh for pity's sake, grow up!, I'm not calling the police, if that's what you're afraid of," said the voice scornfully. "but now that you're here, you might as well make yourself useful. Follow me".

A small woman of mature years, thin, tanned and smoking a cheroot, clad in a white track suit, stepped out of the shadows. Meekly, Norris followed her down the hallway, into another large reception room. It was piled high with boxes, parcels and various pieces of furniture.

"Right, you can load up the van for me, and mind you don't break anything!"

For the next surreal hour, Norris hauled and manhandled the contents of the room into a white van parked in the drive way. The woman said nothing as they worked, though from time to time, Norris heard her swear under her breath, 'Bastard, he'll be sorry!'.

At last, they were finished. She dangled the car keys in front of him.

"Do you want to drive?"

"I can't, I'm only sixteen" he blurted.

"Well, then we're done".

She began to walk away, then stopped, turning slowly to stare at him.

She eyed him speculatively – a singularly unattractive youth with rampant acne and halitosis.

"Actually, there is one thing of his you can have before you go"

He watched in horror as she slowly undressed, revealing her skinny frame wreathed in crepe fake-tanned skin and wizened breasts. She smiled grotesquely.

Norris fainted.

PART 2

THE VISIT

"Hello, son."

"Hi, Dad".

"How's your Mother?"

"Fine".

"Is she still- "?

"Yes".

"How are you?"

"Fine".

"Hmm".

A silence ensued, during which Norris pondered on whether he should tell his Dad about his first job. Best not to, he decided, it could keep. His Dad was a burglar. He wasn't very good at it, either. He was currently resting at Her Majesty's pleasure, in a low security prison, from which it didn't occur to him to escape. Norris was very like his father.

"Dad?"

"Yes, son?"

"Mum's a bit..................a bit more..................well, she's worse."

"Oh".

Another short silence, then-

"Do you want to go to your Aunty Jean's again for a bit?"

"Naw, I'm okay."

"Who is she, this time?"

"Someone called Mary. Mary Archer."

"Oh"

"She's using loads of perfume and says she's a fragrant lady."

"Oh"

"She thinks I'm a spy."

"Oh".

"Dad?"

"Yes, son?"

"I moved out last week. Just until you come home."

"What! Is your mother left on her own?"

"Oh no, no. Aunty Jean 's moved in. She's left Uncle Raymond again."

"What's he done this time?"

"I don't know, but she was going to cut off his...........well, she chased him away, anyway. All through the Saturday market and down Nassau street. He got away over the Bakery wall."

"So, where are you staying, then?"

"Well, it's like I'm a sort of lodger, but I don't pay any money – I do jobs to pay the rent. Near the Primary School."

"What jobs?"

Norris hesitated. He felt reluctant to mention that actually, he was living in a shed, into which he barricaded himself each night. Also, he thought it best not to mention his landlady's white tracksuit, or the cigars. His tenancy was entirely accidental – a choice between a threat of being reported for attempted burglary if he refused to help a 'helpless old lady' who had tracked him down, and a truculent, brooding Aunty Jean, whose uncertain temper was legendary. His Mother's efforts to inform the Queen of his spying activity was the last straw, and so he left home.

"Moving stuff. Painting walls, and cleaning the yard. She's an old woman, she can't manage on her own. And I've got a part time job in Asda, stacking shelves."

"Oh."

His Dad cleared his throat, then spoke again.

"Son"..

"Yes, Dad?"

"Don't go into the trade."

"Oh".

"I'm giving it up, when I get out."

Then he stood up, and waited to be escorted back to his cell.

"Goodbye, son. See you next time."

Norris always felt tearful when his Dad disappeared from view, but this time, he was unusually light-hearted. His Dad had only a few months to go, and Norris skipped along, almost happy.

He turned into his street, but stopped dead. The normally quiet street was crowded with police cars, an ambulance, and pushing, gaping on-lookers. A photographer from the local press was gleefully snapping away, and Norris was horrified when he saw the focus of their attention.

Sitting astride the garage roof, skinny legs dangling, was his landlady, but the white tracksuit was nowhere to be seen, alas. She was singing lustily, waving an empty champagne bottle – and she was entirely naked.

"What's going on? What's she doing on the roof?" Norris asked a man at the back of the crowd.

"Don't know, mate, but she's enjoying herself, anyway".

A woman with a face as bleak as winter, said bitterly,

"Apparently her husband's just died suddenly, and she's getting everything. He must have been worth a bob or two, to make her that happy. Wish mine would do me a favour and drop dead, too."

Another woman eagerly joined the conversation.

"I heard he left her a few weeks ago, but he never mentioned divorce, so she's still his wife, and she gets all his money. And the house."

On the roof, the last tuneless bars of 'Delilah' faded away, and she screamed down at the upturned faces of the crowd.

"Do you know what he was doing when he kicked the bucket?" she yelled.

"He was in bed with his fancy woman, that's what! She killed him in the end, ha! ha!"

She screeched joyfully as the crowd cheered her on, and flung her arms wide, teetering dangerously.

"Look what he's missing!" she yelled.

Norris couldn't stand it any longer. Quickly and quietly, he slipped around the back of the house and down to the shed at the bottom of the garden. He packed up his meagre belongings and left by the back gate, with 'Delilah' ringing in his ears again. He thought he would go home. Things were bound to have settled by now.

As he approached his house, he heard a loud, deep voice singing, slurred but clearly audible. It was Aunty Jean, who had the postman in an inescapable arm lock, serenading him. She had already gone through her rendition of 'Delilah' to assuring him that he was "A lovely wee man" to snarling,

"Men! They're all the same! Bastards!" and the expression on her face turned ugly. She was very drunk, and soon to be very disorderly. She flexed her arm, almost choking the postman who squeaked a terrified "Help!"

Aunty Jean bunched her fingers into a huge fist. She held it close to her captive's face.

"See that?"

Norris knew what would come next. He pitied the postman, but he couldn't help him, so he fled the scene, almost colliding with his Mother, who glided gracefully out of a neighbour's house, from which she had removed such monies and items of worth as she could find. She didn't recognise him.

PART 3

Norris sat in his small green tent. It was pitched in the car park at the back of Asda, by permission of the night security man. It was his third week in the tent. The front flap was open, and he imagined he could see the stars through a cold fog that hung in the air like damp washing, clinging to his face and hair. His thoughts were a little muddled, as he was not only tired and cold, but also alarmed by the increasingly overly familiar attentions of the security man, and the nightly shower of stones which a gang of small boys accurately delivered over the top of the high fence.

Why was everyone he knew crazy, except his Dad? He thought of the white track suit and cigars, and of Aunty Jean. Why did drunk people always sing 'Delilah?' He thought of his Mother, and wondered what she had been like when she was younger – he couldn't remember her when she was well, and must have loved him.

He couldn't stop shivering. A lady from the Health Clinic had visited him a couple of days ago, but he had refused any help, being habitually suspicious of officialdom. Now, he wished he had taken her offer.

He felt cold, so very cold. He thought he might die quietly of hypothermia. Just let go.

He liked that thought.

Gradually, he drifted off into a shallow sleep.

Footsteps, stealthily creeping across the gravel, jerked him awake.

'It's the night security man,' he thought.

What should he do? Pretend to be asleep? Make a run for it? Yell for help? The footsteps stopped at the front of the tent. Someone fiddled with the zip, and Norris called out in a quavering voice

"Who's there?"

The flap opened.

"Go away! Go away!" Norris squawked, as he launched himself blindly towards the opening, desperate to escape. The tent collapsed around him in suffocating folds, and unseen hands pulled at the tent fabric. Then suddenly, Norris stopped struggling, as he inhaled the powerful smell of prison soap.

"It's me, son, it's only me."

"Dad!".

Home at last.

MONKEY SUIT

"Write about what you know", intoned the tutor at the Adult Evening Creative Writing class, and in the small community centre, seven heads bent over their notebooks, scribbling obediently. But the eighth person in the class leaned back in her chair, frowning to herself, quite unable to think of anything at all that she knew anything about. It was stuffy in the small room, the smell of damp coats drying out, vague odours of cooking oil and steamed vegetables, and Ethel felt heavily sleepy.

"Ethel dear, are you not writing?" the tutor enquired archly, and turning to her classroom assistant added in an audible aside, "She's got no imagination, no imagination at all – I don't know why she bothers".

Ethel heard the remark, but it failed to cause her any upset – she thought the tutor was probably right. Turning to stare out of the window into the darkness of a November night, she had a nagging sense that she had forgotten something.

'I've got the bread,' she mused, 'and I've paid the rest of the electric bill – but I'm sure there was something else. Oh well, it'll just have to wait until I'm in the village again, the community bus won't wait when this class is over, and it's too far to walk the whole way home. Anyway, it can't be important if I've forgotten it!'

Almost a year had passed since Ethel's father had died, wheelchair-bound for the last years of his life. At the age of 51, Ethel finally had no-one to answer to. No-one to forbid her to spend money on an ice cream, no-one to swing a heavy cane across her shoulders as she passed the wheel chair, no-one to pour scorn on the idea of her going to an evening class, no-one to tell her she was worthless, useless, stupid, ugly.

It was strange at first, rattling around in the huge old house, and she had just begun to get used to it when Bobby came home, three months after their father had died. He hadn't come to the funeral, but that was hardly surprising, as he hadn't been home for oh, it must have been nearly 30 years. Well, he couldn't come home, could he, after that business of the girl in the car on the way home from a dance. Her brother had blustered and threatened and denied, but for once, he didn't get away with it, so he fled before there was any

retribution meted out. Ethel had been so happy to be free of him, free of......
oh, best not to think about that.

With an effort, she picked up her pen again.'I once had a kitten, it was a tabby...'
Ethel wrote, then she put the pen down, a little perturbed by the memories
awakened by that sentence. The kitten had been a birthday present from her
mother when Ethel was 6 years old, just a couple of weeks before her mother
ran away with the insurance man. After all these years, Ethel still wondered
why her mother had left her behind.

'If she found it too awful to stay, why did she leave me behind?' But there
was never an answer to that question, so there was no point in thinking about
it. Ethel had been at her father's and Bobby's mercy for a long, long time.

'I'm not in the mood tonight', she thought, and for the rest of the class time,
she copied out a favourite childhood poem, having nothing original to write.
Later, as the bus lurched along the country road, Ethel leaned her forehead
against the cold glass of the window, and stared out into the dark, watching
the comforting lights of the village disappearing into the secret folds of the
landscape. As the bus shuddered to a halt at the entrance to the long lane up
to her house, a chorus of 'g'night Ethel!' sounded, then the bus drew away,
and she was left alone in the dark. She didn't mind. Plodding steadily up
the rutted track, she had no torch to light the way, no quivers of fear at her
aloneness, no misgivings as the wind rustled and moved in the hedgerows
closing around her. 'No imagination, that's me!' she had jokingly said, when
asked if she were afraid in that big house, or going up that spooky laneway.
Anyway, many things had already happened to her, in that house when it was
not dark, and she had not been alone – there was little left to fear.

Bobby had come back, he said, to claim his inheritance. He was going to
sell the house, and as everything had been left to him, she would get nothing,
and have nowhere to live. That wasn't the worst part, oh no. It was the way he
eyed her speculatively, his eyes following her around as she went about her
daily routine that unnerved her. It was just a matter of time.

Reaching half way up the steep lane, she paused to get her breath. 'Must be
getting old,' she thought, 'First I'm forgetting things, now I'm out of puff just
going up the lane'.

As she drew breath, unbidden, disquieting thoughts arose that made her
shiver, but she quite firmly and deliberately shut them away. Just as she had
shut Bobby away.

She had never allowed herself to dwell on unpleasant things – that was how she had survived those years, so now she forbade herself to remember that day, when he had been back almost two weeks, and she knew she couldn't escape him much longer. He had ordered her to bring more coal for the fire in the small study, but she wasn't fast enough to please him. He came down the coal-cellar steps, roaring like a bull, anger echoing round the damp, dark walls. In her haste to bring the coal bucket, Ethel tripped on the bottom step, spilling the coal all over the floor. Still roaring, his face contorted, he grabbed the bucket and shovel roughly from her, pushing past her into the little enclosed space where the coal was heaped. Formerly a kennel, there was a metal gate on the doorway, and as Bobby rushed in, his jacket caught on the metal handle, slamming it shut behind him. They both heard the lock click into place, and there followed a small, small, thoughtful silence.

"Open the door!", he bellowed, "Open it now!".

Ethel stood perfectly still.

"Open it! Now! Stupid bitch, you'll pay for this! Open the door!".

Ethel stood perfectly still. She looked at the gate, nicely made metalwork that had no space at the top, to prevent any dogs getting over. She looked at the small enclosure where Bobby stood, rattling the bars furiously. There was a single light bulb dangling precariously near the bottom of the steps, and a dripping tap loosely screwed to the wall beside the gate. A key hung on a hook, just out of her reach, high on the wall.

"But Bobby", she said, in a calm, sweet voice," I can't reach the key!"

Some people claim that your whole life flashes before you in a milli-second at the time of facing death or great danger. Ethel certainly seemed to feel all of hers rushing through her brain and body in a crashing tidal wave, then she became icily calm, disembodied. The loud, fierce yelling faded into a white mist, and she stared around, like an unexpected victor in a previously hopeless battle. She moved a tentative step towards some dishes the dogs used to drink from that were lying on the floor.

Thoughtfully, she dusted one off on her skirt, filled it with water, and slid it within range of the animal in the coal cellar. Grabbing it up, he threw it at Ethel with as much force as he could, and bellowed over and over, "Open this door! Open it!".

The dish shattered against the wall, and Ethel gave a little light laugh.

"Missed!"

Then she turned and went sedately up the steps without looking back, the bellowing and rattling fading away as she closed the door to the cellar at the top step. That night, she slept right through the night for the first time since her mother had left.

At first, Ethel fed the creature in the cellar regularly, bringing down a share of whatever dinner she had made, sliding the plate under the gate with a broom shaft.

She never spoke to him, just came and went when she remembered, but as time went by, she sometimes forgot all about him and he went unfed. How he had shouted and screamed! As the weeks and months passed his cries became a whimper, and lately, just a grunt or two.

He was a dirty beast, though, and the smell in the cellar was disgusting. Ethel didn't relish going down to the cellar at all. She had the coal delivered to the garage, saving herself a lot of heavy carrying. It was cold down there, too, and the creature coughed and shivered.

Searching for something in a cupboard one day, Ethel found a fancy dress costume from long ago – a thick, furry monkey suit, with furry gloves for the hands. Shaking the dust out of it, she thought it would be just the right fit for the cellar occupant, and so warm, so appropriate. Later that day, she pushed it near the bars of the gate, just within his grasp. It was a week or two after that when Ethel began to feed him bananas – after all, they were a quick and handy meal, no cooking needed, and so easy to bring home from the village. Nowadays, he lived on them.

Reaching the house at last, she relaxed for a few moments, before making herself a nice, warming mug of cocoa, then she went contentedly up the stairs to bed. Reflecting on her evening class, she conceded that indeed, she had no imagination, no, none at all. Snuggling cosily under the blankets, a comforting hot water bottle at her feet, she sighed happily. Just as she was dropping off to sleep, she remembered what she'd forgotten to get in the village.

Bananas.

ROBERT ISN'T GOING TO SCHOOL ANYMORE

Robert isn't going to school anymore. He sits at his window in his little room upstairs, listening to his mother in the kitchen below. He hears the busy-ness of her as she moves about from cupboard to cooker, from table to sink. She is purposeful, useful, angry. Robert sighs heavily, shifting his gaze out of the window to the stale familiarity of his bedroom instead. He sees the small hard bed with its faded blue cover, which smells slightly musty when he pulls it up over his chin. The matching curtains are faded to the same nondescript shade, and pulled primly halfway across, so that they provide little privacy, yet let in little light. Everything in his room seems to be out of focus. He tries to concentrate, to feel alert and sharp, but a sluggishness holds him – he wonders if he is having a stroke. Taking deep breaths, he stands up, swinging his arms, blinking, trying to feel real. He looks around the room again. From the muted blur surrounding him, just the piece of rope he carried home from the beach months ago stands out. It looks alive.

Clink. Clink. The dishes are being hounded into cleanliness. The tasks of the morning will soon be finished, and he will no longer be able to avoid her.

Robert lies down on the bed, and makes a conscious effort to breathe slowly, while forcing himself to think. Things seem to swim in and out of focus as he looks around, then the poster stuck on the back of the door becomes clear, showing beautiful brightly coloured birds – flamingos, long-tailed parrots, birds of paradise, toucans, scarlet ibis. He remembers, with an unexpected rush of anguish, the long- ago feel of his father's arms around him as they squashed together in an armchair, reading wonderful stories of distant places – Peru, Tasmania, Ethiopia, Egypt, Madagascar. On their walks, when they had each other all to themselves, they planned marvellous journeys when all the wonders of the world would unfold for them. Robert recalls his long forgotten dreams being swallowed up in 'you're the man of the house now, you'll have to look after your mother', at his father's funeral. Since then, he has stopped hoping to see a toucan in the woods, or hear the cry of peacocks at dawn.

He heaves himself off the bed, and crosses the room to open the window a little. A pleasant spring breeze wafts confidently through, rustling a few papers on the desk, and as he reaches to stop them blowing about, out of the corner of his eye he sees the salt-bleached rope sway languorously.

Looking out again, he sees a couple walking hand-in –hand, school bags weighing them down, absorbed in each other. They sit in front of him in class. They do not trouble him at all, but when they pass by in school, they look right through him, as though he is invisible. Yesterday, even in all the uproar, they remained apart, unmoving, as always. Others pass down the street, glancing furtively at his window, their heads coming closer together as they debate yesterday's debacle. He doesn't care anymore. The stone that lodged in his heart after his father died has disappeared and he feels curiously empty. He is afraid that he may have lost something precious. He closes his eyes and images swirl about in slow motion, chased by fragments of voices, impressions of anger. He cannot stop hot shameful memories of yesterday, and all the other yesterdays he has spent in St. Matthew's High School, gathering pace in the burning dark spaces behind his eyelids. He sways slightly, so that he must stretch his hand blindly to the window-sill to steady himself.

He sees himself in that first year, sure that, at times, he is entirely invisible. Life in school goes on around him daily, as he stands in the corridors or playground, seldom speaking or being spoken to. His recent grief has made him unusually quiet, and so a little different from the other first-formers, but different is dangerous. 'Different' can seem like a provocation to those who rule the times and places outside the restraints of the classroom.

'Different' brings sly kicks, unexpected pushing going through doorways, pencils jabbed painfully into thighs. Later, it becomes a blazer ripped from collar to pocket, homework sheets shredded and scattered over puddles, lunch money prised out of bruised fingers. Finally, it is hard knuckles against the head, arm twisted to breaking point behind the back, boots slamming into the soft flesh of the stomach. The doctor in Casualty purses his lips sceptically when Robert explains that he is just clumsy, it is all his own fault, really. "Everything all right at home, son?" he enquires, but Robert knows what to say – and what not to say. He hears sniggers next day as he passes by with his arm in a sling, and sees the frightened glances of his friends, how they look carefully around to see who may be watching, before they speak to him. Robert understands.

Sweating lightly, pulse surging, Robert finally gives in and allows himself to look at his latest yesterday. He sinks back down onto the chair, the cool rope brushing against his hand suggestively. It begins just like any other day. Jonathan Davis, hero of the football pitch, shoulders him aside as he enters the classroom. Jonathan's cousin, Dave, follows on his heels, literally, scraping a metal-tipped boot down Robert's ankle, declaring with a sneer "Oh! Did that hurt? Sorreeeeee!" Robert carries on to his desk, trying not to limp. On his desk he puts papers and books, but as he bends down to stow away his bag, the desk is rocked from the impact of Charlie Keown cannoning into it, scattering papers on the floor. Charlie's girlfriend, Catherine, slouches along behind, walking over the pages as though she hasn't seen them. She doesn't screw them under her foot to make sure of maximum damage, so Robert hopes it will be a bearable day. He soon knows this is a vain hope when Stevie Doran pauses to fart loud and long in Robert's face as he rises from picking up his papers. Stevie bows theatrically to his mates, who applaud him with gusto, cheering and stamping.

At break time, Robert sits outside alone. He has spent almost all of his life so far in school, and he is idly working out the percentage it represents, when a pleading voice floats tremulously from an open window above. He is not particularly interested, and continues with his calculations. He despises himself for his passive acceptance, then and now – for his belief that coming back would somehow make it all right. He knows that this is the end, he can't carry on anymore, not even for another day.

Suddenly he is aware of the voice again, imploring, "not that! – oh please- don't break that!" The taut cable of endurance finally snaps in his head. Then he is on his feet, running crazily through doors, along corridors, knocking people out of his path. He does not realise that he is roaring like a bull nor note the glass in the door shattering as he bursts into the room. Three startled faces turn towards him, one paler than the others. As he grabs Jonathan Davis by the throat, he kicks Stevie Doran viciously between the legs, and then again, as Doran buckles to the floor, writhing in agony. His hands are vice-like on Davis throat and from far away he hears his own voice bellowing at their victim, "Don't beg them! Never beg! Never ! Never!"

He only vaguely remembers his hands being prised from their grip on Davis, being restrained in the headmaster's office, disconnected words and half sentences whirling in his ears.

"What on earth possessed you……? nearly throttled…..! NO excuse for …unprovoked attack….lucky it's not a murder charge!…immediate suspension…can't believe it… you, a past pupil… newest member of staff… never teach again…safety risk to pupils…my god, such brutality…seemed so …appearances deceptive…my god!"

After the police have taken their statements, he is led from the headmaster's office. He sees Doran crouched whimpering against the wall, his cronies keeping their distance among a sea of gawping faces. There is total silence as Robert approaches. He pauses long enough to expel a huge viscous lump of spittle in Doran's face before he can be hustled away. A lone voice shrills "Good for you, Sir!"

Robert sits at his window in his little room. A magazine lies open on his desk. "Casual Crew wanted" it declares. "Apply North Africa Cruises Ltd." Robert is leaning back in the chair. He feels the rough fibre of the rope, pushing impatiently against his back. In his hand, he holds a picture of a scarlet ibis.

One way or another, Robert isn't going to school anymore.

A BED OF ROSES

"And I'm thinking of writing a book – I might put it on that webnet thingy. What do you think, Rita?"

The gentle rattle of the tea trolley's wheels competed shyly with Shirley's chatter as she entered the cosy sitting room. She had talked all the way from the kitchen, even though she must have known that she couldn't possibly be heard, in that breathy, girly tone that her cousin Rita found quite endearing. Cheeks glowing pink in the warmth, her white hair a soft nimbus around her head, Shirley manoeuvred her pleasantly plump figure around the equally plump furniture, fussing with tinkling china cups, delicate bone-handled spoons. Rita wriggled deeper into the cushioned depths of her chair, content to let the words flow over her, not really listening.

"Central heating is grand, but you can't beat a good coal fire", she declared, seeing Rita's eyelids droop sleepily as she plied her with tasty sandwiches and tiny scones, a feather-light Victoria sponge oozing jam and cream, pretty tray bakes.

"Stanley never let me light a fire in this room, he was too mean. Now, what was I saying?" pondered Shirley, having lost track of her narrative during the pouring out and passing over, then she exclaimed,

"Oh yes – I remember!" Here she paused to balance a piece of fruit bread on the side of her saucer, then went on,

"Now Rita, I've given this considerable thought in the last few years, when he was getting on my nerves so badly, I didn't just rush into it! He was so critical, picking on me for every tiny fault – pick, pick, pick. And oh how he loved to pinch my arm so hard that I was black and blue! Women shouldn't have to live like that, bullied day in, day out. He followed me about the house, never doing anything useful, just going on and on at me. He spoiled everything I enjoyed. I had no peace in the garden, either. He trailed after me there too, yap, yap, yap! How I resisted the urge to bury the spade in the back of his head, I'll never know!"

She poured some more tea for them both, and Rita thought to herself that Shirley hadn't stopped talking since Stanley had left, most of it incomprehensible. He left no forwarding address, and no-one knew where he had gone, though such was his character that he wasn't really missed. It was understood that he was probably staying with his elderly uncle in Scotland.

"Anyway, I thought for a long time, and I just knew I'd have to get rid of him, he was never going to go by his own choice – do you like my new china cabinet? Stanley didn't like clutter, so I bought it after......"..Here Shirley paused thoughtfully, then said, a trifle defiantly, "I've earned his mean old money, haven't I, so I can spend! spend!, can't I?"

A little startled as Shirley's words eventually began to sink in, Rita thought she must have misheard, and she listened more with a little more attention, as Shirley prattled on,

"It's December now, so it was last February ...no, no... it was January......no, it was last February, yes I'm positive it was February, that I tried the poison. I did think it might be a bit painful for him, but then Stanley never cared about making me feel pain, so I decided to try it anyway. It was my first choice."

At this, Rita sat up so violently that she choked on her scone, causing Shirley to thump her vigorously on her back.

"Don't take such big mouthfuls, dear", she chided Rita gently, "Scones can be a bit dry."

"Anyway," she continued, not letting a bit of coughing interrupt her, "I did everything it said on the packet- did I tell you I got it from that big garden centre at the roundabout, they were very kind, they even asked me what it was for! Of course I couldn't tell them what it was really for, oh! maybe that's why it didn't work? Then again, I might have forgotten what they said before I got home."

She broke off to peer intently at Rita, enquiring solicitously,

"You look a bit peaky, dear, are you alright? Have some more tea!"

Without waiting for a reply, Shirley continued, lowering her voice conspiratorially, ignoring Rita's crimson face and ragged breath.

"I tried it on the cat first, and it died, so I can't understand where I went wrong..."

She gave an exasperated little sigh, and paused ever so briefly.

"You know, I spent weeks on that, starting with just a little, and building it up, but he wasn't even a little bit sick, not even once! Do you think I should ask for my money back? Perhaps I've left it a little bit late?"

A small pause ensued, Shirley happily eating a chocolate brownie, Rita transfixed in her chair, frantically thinking, "This can't be true, she wouldn't ....would she?"

"My second choice nearly worked, it was my favourite because I thought it up myself. Guess what it was? Vaseline in the bath!"

Shirley laughed to herself, a strange little laugh that sent shivers up Rita's spine.

"Shall I make us cocktails? Oh lets be really decadent – or is it decorous? Cocktails in the afternoon! What would Stanley say if he knew? He'd be horrified!"

A strangled sound issued from Rita's chair, then she managed to croak out just one word –

"Driving!"

"Poor dear, I forgot about that, never mind, we'll do cocktails some other day. So my idea was really good, and so simple! I smeared the bottom of the bath with Vaseline, just a tiny amount. Well, it should have worked, but it all went wrong. He was supposed to slip and bang his head on the taps and be knocked out. Then I would hold his head underwater until he drowned. I think that would be the most perfect way, no-one would think that I could manage that, but you'd be surprised at how strong I am!"

Flexing her arms, Shirley demonstrated just how capable she could be, and Rita drew ever deeper into her chair, away from those menacing waving arms.

"But it all went wrong! "Shirley shouted, becoming agitated, "All wrong! The old bugger fell alright, but he only broke his leg! I had to spend the next few months looking after him, the bastard! Bastard!"

Making soothing noises, Rita encouraged Shirley back into her chair, acutely aware of the cake knife Shirley brandished in her hand. She couldn't help thinking of the dessert Shirley had made – it was called Death by Chocolate.

"I'm sorry for my bad language Rita, but he wouldn't do anything for himself. He ordered me about all day, and refused to use his crutches, leaning as heavily as he could on me so my back felt as if it were breaking." She smiled artlessly at Rita, and added, "But it's good to have tried, so when I write my book I can give good advice, because I have the experience, you see. Rita dear, you really are a bit off-colour, you should get a tonic from the chemist, it would pick you up in no time."

"You've never been married, Rita," she continued solemnly, "so my book will be no good to you, but you could always recommend it to your friends, couldn't you? Just imagine, I might be a famous author! Or is it authoress?

I'm sure there's a lot of people in real need of this kind of advice – and I've got loads more ideas! Oh! I've just had a thought! I'll have to try all my ideas out first! It's so exciting! It's called research, isn't it? Oh dear, I'll need an awful lot of cats!"

Again she gave a tinkling, chilling laugh, before going on,

"My third choice was a disaster, it was the electric hedge clippers, and I got the idea from those home safety leaflets in the clinic – I read on one of them that you shouldn't get water in the works, so I gave them a good soaking in the bath when Stanley was out. Everything went wrong, there was oil everywhere in the bathroom, and it took me ages to clean the floor. And then, when Stanley got around to doing the hedge – he only did it because I'm not tall enough – all the fuses blew, and the sockets got damaged too, and it cost a fortune to sort it all out! I had a 'water-tight 'alibi, though!" and here Shirley giggled at her little pun, "I would just say I was giving it a good clean!"

Finally Shirley paused, and gave a deep sigh. There was a short silence, broken only by Rita's teacup and saucer rattling steadily in her trembling hand, then off Shirley went again, a little less calm, her voice hard.

"So there he was, still following me around, calling me stupid, pushing me and pinching me. I thought I would forget all about getting rid of him for a while, and just get on with things, like the garden. I had decided to put in a new rose bed, over near the onion patch, so I was digging a trench one Saturday, and of course out he came after me, complaining about me buying new roses, and I hadn't even bought them yet! Talk about verbal abuse! He had a filthy tongue in his head – thirty seven years with him, and each one worse than the last – and he still hadn't run out of names to call me. He said it wasn't deep enough, him that never did a hand's turn in the garden. Thirty seven years! Thirty seven bloody years!"

Shirley was shouting again by now, a piece of Victoria sponge shredded by her agitated fingers, cake crumbs flying everywhere.

"I said it was deep enough, and I can tell you, I was getting really cross. I had a whole heap of good horse manure – I got it from Dorothy, did I tell you her daughter's going to the R.D.S., or is it U.C.D.? and I wanted to get it in before teatime, but he gave me an ignorant shove and got into the trench, then he said it was too deep! Thirty seven years, thirty seven miserable years – oh God! Thirty seven years! And suddenly I had the spade in my hands – and I was thinking, I can't live like this until I die, I've already wasted thirty seven years! And I was swinging the spade and swinging the spade and swinging the spade – my eyes were shut, I couldn't stop, and then the next thing I knew, I was filling in the trench with all that lovely manure, and there was peace in the garden!

I didn't plant roses after all, I put in a raised potato bed instead.

Isn't that ironic........or is it erotic?...that after such considerable thought, it was just my fit of bad temper that did it in the end?

Oh, are you going so soon, dear? Wait a minute, I'll get you some potatoes to take with you – they're the tastiest I've ever grown!"

THE ETIQUETTE OF BURGLARY

SILENT SPINNING

Dee is standing on the cliff at Carrick Point, almost exactly at the spot where she pushed her grandmother off, six years ago. She is remembering the slow, slow, spinning of the old lady, her clothes fanning out like tattered black wings as she meets the rocks below. It is very satisfying.

She is suitably, convincingly hysterical. What a lot of attention she gets!

'A dreadful thing for a twelve year old to witness!'

When her baby brother Lewis, still strapped in his pushchair, falls noisily from the same spot two years later, it is not particularly satisfying. He screeches all the way down in an erratic, twisting flight. It is all over too quickly. There is no attention, only unspoken suspicion.

Nicholas lies on the rocks below. The sea moves hypnotically back and forth, licking greedily at his still form. How beautifully, silently he fell. He should not have told her their romance is over while strolling along the cliff path. The sound of a distant siren carries on the air. There will be accusation this time.

Dee stands on the edge of the cliff at Carrick Point, poised for flight.

She is totally satisfied.

BIG

Salty sweat trickled into the folds of Christina's skin and she dabbed at herself with a tissue, conscious of the damp patches under her arms, staining the fabric of her dress. The fine silk material clung to her body, emphasising her ample breasts. The train moved jerkily out of the station, packed to capacity with weary commuters suffering in the humid heat of July in the city. She was lucky to get a seat. Staring out of the window, she was unaware of the man sitting opposite her. His gaze was fixed on the deep 'v' of creamy smooth skin between her breasts, and as she folded her arms, he watched her more openly, as the rounded softness was pushed upwards voluptuously.

The rhythm of the train rocked her into a half – doze. She would give Phillip an ultimatum – he would have to leave his wife now. She was angry, not just with Phillip for cancelling yet another date, but also with herself for getting into a situation she had despised others for – being the 'other woman'.

Watching her, the man opposite saw her absorbed in her thoughts. He felt that he could reach over and touch her, and she would never know. He leaned forward, but before he could move any further, the train slowed and she began to gather up her belongings. She stood up, holding onto the pole near the door, the full length of her body languid against the cool metal, swaying as the train came to a stop.

Christina stepped off the train onto the platform. Up the steps, through the turnstile. Nearly home, just a short walk through the small park behind the school. The man didn't hesitate, but hurried off the train, following her at a distance. When she turned into the park, he gloated at the opportunity that had presented itself. He knew this area well, and he anticipated the next few minutes with heightened excitement, his arousal straining against the fabric of his trousers.

Christina heard his footsteps behind her, heard his ragged breathing. 'Another jogger' she thought, and stepped to the side to let him pass. He drew level with her, but instead of jogging on past, he lunged at her, pushing her into the thick undergrowth. His right hand grasped her neck, squeezing hard, the other grabbing at her breasts as she fell to the ground. Shock held her, her body and mind rigid with fear, unable to scream as he squeezed her throat even harder. He pushed his face into her breasts, drooling, muttering lewd words. Easy. She was going to be easy. He started to undo the zip on his trousers with one hand, and suddenly, Christina snapped out of her initial shock. Enormous anger welled up in her. How dare he! How dare he!

Christina was not a small person. She raised one furiously clenched fist and punched him as hard as she could in the eye. His hands instinctively flew to protect his face, and he snarled,

"You'll pay for that, bitch!"

But another punch made him howl in pain, and Christina managed to get to her feet. A raised knee crunched him painfully in the groin, knocking him backwards, her hands clawing at his face, nails raking down his skin. She began kicking him furiously, screaming all the while,

"Bastard! You bastard! You bloody bastard! You bloody men are all the same!"

He tried to get away but she kicked him in the face, the toe of her shoe catching his right eye, so he curled up into a ball to try to protect himself, as she kicked harder. Gradually, she realised that he had stopped moving.

It was quiet, so quiet.

"I hope I've killed him, the dirty bastard!" she thought.

She reached down and grabbed his hair, pulling his head back as roughly as she could. She looked into his face. His eyes were shut, bloodied where she had kicked him. She studied him for a few seconds. He was a slim, sandy-haired man, probably in his thirties. His hair was neatly cut, his clothes unremarkable, ordinary. He could be anyone's father, anyone's brother, respectable, despicable.

She took out her mobile phone, and as she dialled a number, wondered if he would have attacked her if he had known she was an off-duty policewoman.

He groaned, and opened his eyes.

"I'll sue you, fat bitch – I'll sue you for assault" he gasped, clutching his stomach.

"Shut up! Shut your dirty mouth!" Christina warned. She realised that he was recovering, and prayed that someone would come soon. He leered up at her, saying

"I can see up your dress, I can.........."

"Shut up!" Christina screamed, but then a siren wailed, coming closer, car doors slammed, footsteps hurried along the path, and suddenly she was no longer alone. As he was led away, he kept up a stream of vile sexual innuendo, but his parting words were, 'I'll sue you!'

Christina vomited painfully. Her legs buckled beneath her, and she sat on the grass verge, shaking.

"It's Christina, isn't it ?" asked one of the policewomen, putting her hand gently on Christina's shoulder. Christina nodded, her throat raw.

"Can he really sue me?" she rasped.

"No, no don't worry about that. He can try, but those marks on your neck and arms tell their own story. C'mon, let's get you to a doctor."

****

The door clicked shut behind her, and Christina dropped her bag on the floor. Home at last. It was past midnight. She desperately wanted to phone Phillip, but that was impossible. He would be gone in the morning for his annual summer break with his family, and she could not risk arousing suspicion by phoning so late. Who else could she ring? Her affair with Phillip had distanced her from her friends. Her parents were happily retired, living in Portugal, but she would not want to worry them, anyway. That left her younger sister, just a few miles away. Without thinking, she dialled the number.

"Hello?" a breathless voice answered.

"It's me, Christina. Sorry for ringing so late, but........"

"What the hell are you doing, ringing so late?" her sister interrupted. "The baby's only just gone back to sleep, and Francesca's got head lice from some kid at school. and Brian's just told me he wants to give up his job to go travelling, he says we married too young. Who's going to pay the mortgage? I think he's having an affair, he's been out since just after 8, he hasn't phoned, so where the hell is he?"

She paused at last to enquire, "What did you want, anyway?"

"Oh nothing, I didn't realise it was so late. I'll ring you in a few days, ok?"

"Ok". The phone went dead, and Christina thought that was just how she felt. Dead. She made herself go into the kitchen, make a coffee, rummage in the fridge for something to eat, but her throat was too sore, she couldn't swallow. She felt dirty and realised her dress was torn, her hair dishevelled, so she had a long hot shower, scrubbing her skin red and raw everywhere he had touched her. She had dealt with the aftermath of assault in the course of her job, but she felt detached and numb as she went through the process herself. Statements, medical examinations, offers of counselling, numerous cups of tea – it was all a tangle in her head.

She felt exhausted, but instead of going to bed, moved restlessly about the apartment from room to room. She kept going over the attack in her mind, wondering if she had been dressed too skimpily, or somehow caught her attacker's eye by some gesture or look. Was it her fault? Maybe she shouldn't have gone through the park? Finally, she fell asleep on the sofa, the television flickering, the sound a small comfort, as though there was someone else in the room.

****

Christina woke, the sound of her phone ringing somewhere amongst the folds of the blanket she had pulled over her last night. She fumbled about, half asleep, and finally found it. She glanced at her watch, and saw it was almost three o'clock. The station sergeant's voice sounded tired, as he said

"I'll come straight to the point, Christina. It's bad news, he's going to sue. His solicitor thinks he can get him off the assault charges if he lays the same charge against you. I think this is a tactic to draw attention away from the more serious charge of attempted rape"

"What! How can he get away with that? Oh I can't believe this!"

"Well, apparently, because you defended yourself very vigorously, his solicitor is making a big deal of that. He's claiming that you attacked him while he was urinating in the bushes – he does have a good collection of bruises and cuts to show. Also, he maintains that you were trying to flirt with him on the train, ...Christina, are you there still?"

There was silence for a few seconds, then she whispered,

"Is he out? Is he?"

"Well, since it's a case of your word against his, and he didn't actually ...."

Christina broke in sharply,

"Is he?"

"Yes".

Christina's life, from that one word being uttered, changed completely. When the case came to be heard, she felt humiliated and sick as he gave his evidence, but the hardest thing was that she was penalised for 'defending herself rather too vigorously', and the case was dismissed for inconclusive evidence. She could not believe it, She was given an extended term of sick leave, and a few sessions with a counsellor, then left to her own devices.

She had always considered herself to be confident, unafraid, but now, she seldom ventured out. On the few occasions when she did go out, she kept thinking he would appear in a shop beside her, leering triumphantly. Her self image changed, and she began to loath her body, dieting too severely in an effort to make herself less noticeable. She had always had large breasts, and was proud of them, but now she was so conscious of them, that she resolved to have a breast reduction.

Phillip had enjoyed his affair with Christina. She had been fun, bright and bubbly, sexy. He had no intention of leaving his wife, though, Christina's life outside the bedroom was of no interest to him, he was only interested in her body. Since the attack, she only met him at her apartment, which suited him, but she had ceased to be fun. He thought she had become clingy, needy, and he began to think he would move on. There were plenty more girls to be had, without problems, who would be more fun.

One evening, when he was rushing to get home, pulling on his clothes as soon as they had sex, she tried to make him stay a little longer, wanting to talk.

"Oh, for pity's sake, what is there to talk about?" he said, pushing past her out of the bedroom. Christina tried to keep back her tears, and pleaded with him, hating herself but unable to stop.

"I need you to be here for me, don't you realise how it is for me? My heads all over the place. I'm even thinking of getting a breast reduction........."

But before she could say anymore, he said tightly,

"Ok, that's it! I'm sick of you whinging on and on, poor you, poor you. And now you're getting a breast reduction? Can't you see, I'm only here because of them! I'm out of here now, Christina, it's over!"

Then he was gone.

Weeks passed, and Christina bitterly resented the way her life had changed. She felt victimised, and her resentment grew, focusing on the man who attacked her, and then got away with it. She believed he was the cause of Philip leaving her, of her loss of self worth, that somehow, he had a power over her. It was easy for her to find out where he lived, and she began to observe him, monitoring his movements each day. He liked to loiter on quiet pathways, particularly the towpath, always alone, and a plan formed in her mind. She spent days picking her spot, and finally, she was ready – ready for revenge.

It all went wrong.

She had hidden herself among some bushes, intending to take him by surprise. She had only wanted to frighten him, to pretend she was going to push him into the canal. She jumped out in front of him, but she was taken aback by the fear on his face, and the way he cowered in front of her, clearly terrified. He was smaller than her, and as she took a step closer to him, he backed away, blubbering. She was disgusted with herself that she had allowed such a pathetic creature to cause her to feel worthless, and she gave him a little shove of dismissal – he wasn't worth the bother.

Off balance, he fell backwards into the murky water, without making a sound.

"Oh God! I didn't mean that to happen. Oh no!"

She stared at the water, willing him to surface, but the surface remained still and dark. Frantically, she searched for something to prod the murky water with. Wrenching a long stick from the hedge, she stirred it about, hoping to feel something, someone, catching it, but nothing, no-one appeared. She heard voices, and quickly threw the stick away.

There was nothing she could do. She walked back the way she had come, meeting nobody on the path. She slowed her pace down, breathing deeply. Near the bridge, she paused, getting her breath back, and that was when she saw him.

Phillip was emerging from the Bridge Bar, his head thrown back, laughing. He was so handsome. His arm was around a blonde girl who clung to him, wearing a tight white dress that clearly showed her voluptuous figure. Her heart filled with jealousy and longing.

He still had the power to wound her, and it was then that Christina realised she had killed the wrong man.

PERFECTLY LOVELY

Adrienne glanced smugly around the classroom. Her dark glossy curls bounced, her piercing blue eyes noting every move her classmates made, as she arranged her books tidily on her desk. Adrienne, winner on every sports day, top of the class in everything. Adrienne, eleven years old today, prettiest girl in the school.

Adrienne, teacher's pet.

She frowned as she noticed Marie's silken blonde hair fall softly over the flawless skin of her face. Shy Marie, who had just broken one of Adrienne rules. There were a lot, and the first one was that Adrienne was in charge.

"Don't have anything to do with her!" she would order. "She has nits!". "Keep away from Karen – she's stupid!". "We hate Lucy, she's stuck up!". "We don't play with boys, they stink!"

It was this last rule that Marie had broken, laughing as the boy sitting next to her pulled a funny face. Adrienne waited until break-time, when she pushed Marie against the wall, knocking the breath from her.

"Don't think you can get away with talking to the boys – I saw you! You won't be coming to my party after school!" Then she flounced away to divide and conquer elsewhere.

Marie would have been very pleased to avoid going to the party, but she knew, with sinking heart, that she would have to. Adrienne would be unable to resist showing off the presents, the food and the juggler who was to entertain the guests, most of whom were aware of the consequences of not attending. So, later, Marie's mother would deliver her timid daughter unknowingly into Adrienne's domain along with all the others, none of whom would dare to tell. Adrienne, confident dictator, ruled unopposed.

However, as Christmas approached in this final year of Primary school, Adrienne's world was rocked by an unthinkable event. Despite the fact that Adrienne knew beyond doubt that she was the obvious choice, she was not given the most coveted part in the nativity play. Bottom of the class, stupid, shy, can't be heard behind a newspaper Marie, was to play the part of Mary. The part for the prettiest girl.

Adrienne's part.

"You can't even act!" she stormed, after the first rehearsal.

"You're so stupid, you'll forget the words! You've only been allowed to do it because they feel sorry for you, because you're so thick!"

She threatened, cried, then threatened some more, but the decision was not in Marie's hands. She had a minor part as the inn-keeper's wife, and try as she might, she was unable to upstage Marie. Her heart hardened as she watched Marie in the company of the others in the play, unable to stop the conversations that she had not sanctioned, the laughter she had not initiated.

The weeks and months rolled by, and it was time for the bewildering first year of secondary education, with it's sea of unfamiliar faces, labyrinth corridors and endless rules. Adrienne was thoroughly unsettled, as she was in the top stream, with none of her former classmates. Nobody knew who she was, nobody was in awe of her, nobody cared. On the first day, during break, she sought out Marie. She found her chatting happily to girls – and boys – who did not know her rules. She gripped Marie's arm with spiteful fingers, dragging her to one side.

"What do you think you're playing at?" she hissed. "We don't know these people! How dare you leave me to look for you, you should be glad I'm still hanging around with you, you stupid thing!".

Somehow, Marie found the courage to stand up for herself.

"I'm in a different class to you now – it's not the same anymore!"

For her temerity, Marie had her ears soundly boxed, after which Adrienne flounced away, sneering over her shoulder,

"Don't come crawling to me when everyone finds out what a loser you are! Get lost!".

Marie thought a red welt on her cheek and a stinging ear was a small price to pay for her freedom, for after that, apart from spiteful remarks or an occasional sharp shove or kick, Adrienne left Marie alone.

Term followed term, year followed year. Adrienne became, once again, top of her class. She excelled on the sports field, and played in the school orchestra. However, her pretty face never quite blossomed into beauty, hampered by the canker of envy that lodged in her spirit towards Marie.

Blissfully unaware of the depth of Adrienne's feelings, Marie, too had some small successes, but her compassionate nature was her most attractive quality. By her seventeenth year, she possessed an inner beauty perfectly complimented by outer loveliness. Boyfriends had become the must-have accessory for many of her classmates, but Marie, still shy, remained uninterested.

Until she noticed Mark. Mark was quiet and studious, with dark brown eyes. She stole glances at him when she could, but if he happened to catch her eye, she would look quickly away, her face flooding with colour. She let herself dream of unlikely scenarios when he would sit beside her on the bus, or walk her home, or take her for a coffee. She could never envisage him speaking to her, and she played these innocent silent movies over and over in her head.

Someone else had also noticed him. Adrienne's predatory eye had fallen on Mark, and she made every effort to make him notice her. She sat beside him during music practice, followed him to lunch, talked ceaselessly to him about their English literature project, but to no avail. He was polite, but he barely noticed her.

Mark boarded the bus one cool autumn morning, determined to speak to the blonde girl whose eye he had been trying to catch for months. He made his way to where she sat and leaning over, asked quietly,

"Do you mind if....?" Indicating the empty seat beside her, letting the sentence trail away. She shook her head, blushing furiously. They journeyed in silence all the way to school, Mark desperately trying to think of something to say. Just before they arrived, Marie turned to him, and smiled, a wide, encouraging smile. Breathless, he managed to ask, "Meet you after school? At the bus stop?". She nodded, then they both went off to class, to will the hours away until they would meet.

Marie's friends teased her gently as her relationship with Mark flourished. When they met in the crowded corridors, people and sounds flowed around them unheeded, as they only had eyes for each other. Adrienne watched Mark. She watched Marie.

Stupid Marie.

Beautiful Marie.

With her Mark.

She planned the attack carefully. She stalked Marie until she was sure that Marie was in the locker room alone. Marie turned in surprise as the door crashed open, then backed away in terror, as Adrienne flew at her, screaming, "Bitch! I'm going to ruin you!" She brandished a pair of sharp scissors in one hand, and grabbed Marie's long fine hair with the other. "This will teach you to steal other people's boyfriends!" she snarled, hacking at the hair, pulling out more than she was cutting, such was the force of her anger. Marie put her arms up to shield herself, and felt the sharp blades slice into her flesh.

She tried her hardest to evade Adrienne's grasp, and at last pulled away from her, to stagger out into the corridor, where she fainted. Adrienne strode out behind her, and throwing the scissors down with a contemptuous gesture, walked calmly away.

If Adrienne had hoped that cutting off Marie's hair would make Marie unattractive to Mark, she was sadly mistaken. With her hair re-styled into a fetching gamine, Marie looked more beautiful than ever. The wound in her arm healed, leaving only a tiny scar. Adrienne showed no remorse, and was expelled.

Mark and Marie were a couple. All through Mark's university years, they treasured the times they had together, and planned to marry as soon as Mark graduated. Marie worked in her parent's small bakery, and forgot all about Adrienne.

Adrienne did not forget about her. She eventually qualified as a teacher, and secured a good position, which allowed her to afford a fine life-style. Still, in the depths of her soul, she held an unwavering hatred for Marie. Sometimes, she took that hate out of it's dark place and savoured it, but mostly it lay dormant, a malign memory.

It was the day of Marie and Mark's wedding. The sun shone in through the stained glass of the church, touching their bowed heads as they exchanged vows, like an ethereal blessing. After the ceremony, they walked hand-in-hand down the aisle, and into the sunshine, standing in a shower of rice and confetti, the perfect couple. In the street, traffic slowed to watch.

On this most wonderful day for Marie, Adrienne was having a disastrous day.

Adrienne loved her job. In the classroom, she kept tight control, and frequently reduced even the toughest pupils in her class to tears. She was proud of that. When the post of head of department became vacant, she applied, confident that she was the best candidate. However, not only was the position awarded to someone else, but Adrienne was summoned to appear before the school Board of Governors, to answer a charge of emotional child abuse. She was astounded to hear the charge, brought by the parents of a child in her class. She expected to have the backing of the Principal, but found herself alone in her own defence. She could barely conceal her contempt for the proceedings, and finally lost her temper.

"Your child is a stupid, ill-mannered moron! Now that I've met you, I know why!" she shouted at the unfortunate parents who were in attendance. There was uproar after that, which resulted in the Principal calling security staff to escort Adrienne from the building, saying gravely to her, "I'm bound to tell you that, as of now, you are suspended." Adrienne screamed with impotent fury, as she was coerced none too gently into her car. She revved the engine, and drove furiously away, swearing and shouting. It took her only a few minutes to reach the main street, and she was still agitated, breathing heavily, blind with fury. She failed to notice the traffic slowing as she neared the church, and slammed into the car in front.

The windscreen shattered, broken diamonds of glass falling all over her, while the hiss of escaping water from the radiator sounded in her ears like a sibilant curse. Adrienne banged her hands on the steering wheel in shock and disbelief.

"Nothing ever goes right for me! What's going on? Why are these idiots stopping?" she screamed. She glanced to her left, and suddenly it all became clear to Adrienne. She saw Marie's lovely face, smiling for the photographer, saw the smiles of the wedding guests. She saw, too, the curious stares around her as she stepped from her car, a trickle of blood running down her face. She brushed aside the concern of the occupant of the car she had run into, and all around her seemed to fade away, voices distant, faces blurred. She saw only Marie. Crystal clear. Turning swiftly to the car again, she plunged her hands into the broken glass. Sharp, glittering crystals, like her eyes. She held them in her clenched fists, lifted them up like an offering. Blood oozed out from between her grasping fingers and the on-lookers backed away in horror. Half-crouching, she ran towards the church door. Marie had her back to her, but she turned, just as Adrienne sprang forward with an animal growl, to crush the broken glass into the perfect loveliness of Marie's face.

A TOUCAN IN THE WOODS

A dragonfly, with huge heavy head, zig-zagged across the narrow tree-lined track, shimmering in the dappled light. Thomas stopped to watch the iridescent whirring wings, and the erratic movements he was sure were caused by its having such a large head on a thin light body. His upper lip, his forehead, and his back where his rucksack clung too snugly to him were damp with sweat. It was hot, and as he moved off again, little puffs of dust exploded silently at each footstep. He had been walking for what he was certain was an entire day, and it occurred to him that soon, the sun would be going down and the jungle would be teeming with dark-time life – and death.

He walked on a little further, and reached a small clearing, with an inviting tree-stump begging to be sat upon. Carefully, he inspected it for bull ants, black widow or red-backed spiders and several possible species of snake, before sitting down with a small sigh of relief. Divesting himself of the rucksack, he took a small sip from his water-bottle, aware that dehydration can creep upon one all too easily.

An amateur entomologist of some considerable experience, despite his youth, he withdrew his notebook and pen from the rucksack and began to make notes. He painstakingly recorded his observations on the flight of the dragon-fly, and included a small sketch of its tilted body. His drawing failed to please him and he resolved to improve his artistic skills before his next trip. He also noted various plants encountered along the way, many unknown to him, which he was careful not to touch. There had been a poisonous-looking vine with blossoms like white trumpets coiled sinuously around trunks and branches, in places hanging lazily down, swaying a little as he passed. It almost seemed as if it had tried to reach out to slyly caress his skin. Shrinking from it's evil touch, he had made himself as thin as possible as he hurried by.

It was pleasant to be resting in the drowsy heat. He tilted his face to the sun, and reached down for his water-bottle which he had placed beside his foot, when his hand made slimy contact with something soft and sticky. Flinging the bottle away from him, he leapt up in horror. He staggered back a few paces, staring at the bottle, on which he could see something black and loathsome – "a leech, it must be a leech!" – he thought. A little less alarmed now, for leeches are not known for their ability to move quickly, Thomas stood quietly in the clearing, allowing his breathing to return slowly to normal. As he stood there, still, he could feel the heart-beat of the jungle, absorb it's measured throbbing into his body, hear the clicking, the whirring, the tickling of beetles, the brush of tiny moths, the saw-like "bizzzz" of intrusive mosquitoes, all loud in his ears. The languid air seemed liquid, as streams of light illuminated golden dust-motes floating, going nowhere in a barely visible dance.

Moving quietly back to his seat, Thomas was conscious of the need for vigilance, feeling the eyes of unseen, unknown creatures upon him. He reached into his rucksack for his lunch, and ate heartily, checking from time to time for any extra meat which might have lodged in his sandwiches. Finishing, his mouth felt dry and his throat a little raw, but he decided against retrieving the water-bottle despite his thirst.

Checking his watch, Thomas was alarmed to find that it seemed to have stopped. This created a problem – how far had he travelled, and how long would it take to get back to camp before sundown? He looked up to the sky, trying to gauge the time by the position of the sun, but an even more menacing sight met his eyes as he gazed into the painful glare. Circling lazily above, several large dark shapes rode on thermals, looking down, down to where he stood, waiting for him to become unmoving. Waiting, waiting. It was impossible to identify the birds due to the blinding sun, but Thomas knew that vultures descend as soon as their prey seems quiescent, so he shook his fist defiantly skywards, daring them to come closer.

The place which had been so pleasant now seemed to come alive with malice. Gathering together his notebook and other belongings, he winced at a spiteful bite from a persistent mosquito. Stepping back a little as he placed things in the rucksack, he both felt and heard the sickening crunch as he trod heavily on a huge green-black dung beetle. Sweating freely now, he fumbled with straps and fastenings as around him the humming, buzzing, creeping, watching, breathing, reached a malevolent crescendo. Stumbling, staggering, he fled from the place, the mocking cry of the huge birds sharp in the air behind him.

With a sibilant hiss, like a wind in the lofty branches above him, a poisoned arrow narrowly missed his ear. A low rumble from the throat of a hungry lion, sounding uncannily like a distant tractor, came distinctly from the tangled creepers on his left. On he rushed, until he suddenly collided painfully with the tree-trunk disguise of a solitary giraffe. It stood stock-still, too surprised to move, so Thomas carefully retreated a few cautionary paces and stopped, ragged gasping breaths tearing his chest. His first solo safari was testing his nerve. Realising his survival depended on a cool head, he set off again at a more sensible pace, alert for predators in the thick undergrowth, or scorpions on the path. Ever the scientific explorer, he made mental note of every animal and bird he saw, resolving to write up his observations later. The vegetation thinned, the threatening, tangled jungle unravelled into familiar woodland. Presently, he arrived at a point where the trees gave way to sweeping grassland, and in the distance a cottage nestled peaceably in the fold of the earth. A tractor trundled about in the yard, and a figure, remarkably like his mother, was hanging washing on a line.

Thomas paused, savouring the last few moments of a successful journey. Gazing back for one last look into the trees, his eyes suddenly widened in surprise. He saw the bird clearly, identified it instantly, absolutely, beyond any doubt. Excitedly, he shook off his rucksack, scrabbled about for pen and notebook – this sighting was too important to wait until later and he wanted to record it immediately. Laboriously, he wrote,

"Saw a Toucan in the woods."

Then he put on the rucksack for the last time and started down the hill towards the house. As he walked through the long soft grass, a hushing wind moved over it, making it whisper lightly, swaying into wonderful patterns under the gentle brushstrokes of the breeze.

DAN THE BREAD

"One white and two brown – and don't be all day! And for heaven's sake, don't lose the change!"

His mother's voice followed Daniel as he trotted away from the cottage door, but as the curve in the lane took him out of her view, he slowed to a walk, then to a dreamy saunter. After the summer shower, puddles steamed gently in the mid–morning heat,treacherous pot-holes in the rough lane hiding their true depth. Dan The Bread would not venture down to the cottage in his van, so Daniel was dispatched to wait for his namesake at the road.

Sometimes, Daniel took so long that Dan The Bread would arrive before him, tooting the horn to hurry him along. Daniel would break into a frantic run, afraid that Dan The Bread would roar away in a cloud of dust, but he never did. He would be standing at the back of the van, pulling the shelves out, pushing loaves about, whistling through his broken front tooth with a faintly hissing noise. He always addressed Daniel with a verbal flourish-

"Well now, Master Daniel, what does she want to-day?"

When so grandly titled, Daniel felt somehow older than his ten years, a Person, not a child. When all the transactions were complete, and Dan The Bread was about to slide the shelves back into the van, he would casually remark-

"There's a bap rolled loose out of that pack, would you mind takin' it? Sure it'll only go to waste!"

Sometimes, it might be a current bun, or best of all, a coconut–covered snowball, perhaps a bit stale, but delicious all the same.

"Two white and one brown, two white and one brown",

Daniel paused to consider-

"Two brown and one white – or two white and one brown?"

Dawdling along, Daniel came to a dog-leg in the lane, where in the distance, he could see the road.

No sign of the yellow van –' oh good, no need to hurry yet.' The thick hedges on each side still held some remnant of white blossom, and a drift of tiny fragrant petals fell around him in the drowsy warm air. He breathed in the delicate scent – but at the sound of a hoarse 'toot-toot', he broke into a run, stumbling in the hard baked ridges of mud.

Dan the Bread watched the small figure in the distance for a moment, then heaved his considerable bulk out of his seat, glad to get away from the oppressive heat in the confines of the cab. Pulling a crushed hankerchief from the pocket of his floury brown overall, he mopped his brow and reached back into the cab for the bottle of water tucked beside the seat. He took a long, satisfying draught, then jamming the bottle back in it's place, he ambled around to the rear doors.

Almost there. As Daniel ran along, puffing heavily in the heat, perspiration gathered across his forehead,trickling saltily into his eyes, down his nose, and on to his lips. He flung an arm in a wiping arc over his face, and oh! he felt the precious coins slide from his clammy hand. A forbidden word burst from him, and scrabbling in the dust for the money, he glanced guiltily over his shoulder, just in case.

A grinding screeching crash cut savagely into the hot indolence of the day. Two cars, speeding along the quiet country road in opposite directions, failed to avoid each other as they came too suddenly on the bread van, tucked onto the grass verge.

For a few shocked seconds, a frightening silence hung in the air. Daniel looked up, his grubby hand stilled, coins forgotten.

Dan the Bread peered cautiously around the back of the van.

A slow creaking from the red coupe facing him,a crumpled door opening, a slender leg tentatively finding the ground, then Dan the Bread reeled back as the leg was followed by a furious whirl of turquoise and yellow silk, accompanied by the staccato sound of high heels stabbing furiously towards the other car. A matronly lady, giving every outward appearance of gentility, sat in her Range Rover with an emphatically unladylike litany streaming from her lips through the open window. The car door gave a half-hearted squeal of protest as it was wrenched open, the high-heeled driver gaining first advantage in a series of shrieking incoherent accusations.

"Just what do you think you're doing, driving like that? Look – just look – you've ruined my car! That'll take hundreds to fix!"

Gathering her wits, Range Rover lady rallied quickly to launch her attack. Stepping purposefully from her seat, she towered over her opponent by a stately six inches. In a swiftly regained sense of verbal refinement, she loudly proclaimed, in rich plummy tones –

"How dare you accuse me of bad driving? This is clearly your fault."

"My fault? My fault? You blind old bat! People your age shouldn't be allowed on the roads! Who do you think you are?"

"Unlike you, you cretinous little scrubber," snarled the matron nastily, "I am entirely certain of my parentage, and know exactly who I am. Now get out of my way while I take statements from the witnesses."

Pointing dramatically at Dan the Bread, she declared "He saw it all!"

Dan the Bread tried to stammer a faint denial, but his words were swallowed up in another shrieking tirade from the younger woman.

"Don't you patronise me, snobby cow! You think you're so smart – well, I've got a witness, too!"

Daniel, who had sidled unobtrusively alongside the bread van, found himself squirming in the painful, pinching grip of the red coupe driver. As she vigorously and vociferously challenged her opponent, gesticulating wildly, Daniel was shaken back and forth like puppet on an exceedingly spiteful string.

"Witness! That under-age yokel! I think not!" responded the older combatant, but before she could continue, Daniel suffered another shaking as his captor answered with-

"Better than a short-sighted old dodderer in a filthy old coat!".

Dan the Bread did not consider himself old. Indeed, he was looking forward to an active, action-packed retirement. But, more importantly, he was deeply offended to be described as 'dirty'. He resolved to enter the fray, and manfully sought to raise his voice high enough to be heard, shouting,

"Ladies! Enough! There's only one way to resolve this – I'll send the boy up the lane to call the police!".

"The police!" shrieked two horrified voices in unison, and two faces turned towards Dan. Daniel was unceremoniously cast aside, as the owner of those thin fingers remembered with rage and frustration the many points on her driving license.

The matron, meanwhile, recalled with dismay the third sherry she'd accepted at Marjorie's morning bridge session just a short time ago, not to mention the brandy she'd had following an acrimonious encounter with the gardener regarding his wages earlier.

"Well, come now", she blustered, "surely this can be resolved in a more appropriate manner".

With relief, the coupe driver inwardly agreed but, not wishing to capitulate suspiciously early, demurred for a few seconds, eventually declaring magnanimously,

"I'm sure that at your age, you'd lose your license – I'm not the vindictive type"

The matron bristled angrily, but knew herself defeated, as she stepped back a little lest anyone could catch a whiff of her morning refreshment.

But, what to do with the witnesses?

As the two drivers advanced purposefully on Dan the Bread and Daniel, the hapless pair shrank back against the bread van. The matron bared her teeth in a parody of a smile, and stopped in front of Dan the Bread. She drew a plump wallet from a pocket, rifled reluctantly in it, then handed him a satisfying wad of notes, saying grandly, "For your trouble – " adding menacingly "and I don't want to see or hear of you again".

The younger driver retrieved her designer handbag from her car, and approached Daniel as though he were some form of alien life. Handing him a small bundle of notes, she opened her mouth to speak. Then, with the disturbing echo of the word 'bribery' ringing in her head, retreated quickly to her crumpled but drivable vehicle.

Seconds later, they were both gone.

Dan the Bread went to the back of the van, thoughtfully tucking the money in his breast pocket. Daniel followed. Dan the Bread rummaged around, confused, for a moment or two. Then he handed Daniel two brown and one white – or perhaps two white and one brown. They regarded each other silently for a few seconds. Dan the Bread cleared his throat, as though he were about to speak, but instead, reached once more into the van. Wordlessly, he handed Daniel a whole packet of soft, fresh, coconut-covered snowballs, then climbed into the van and waited, as he always did, for Daniel to begin his short journey home.

LOOKING AFTER COLIN

I like looking after Colin.

I thought I'd resent it, day in, day out, after he had his stroke, but I don't mind, really. When they told me that he'd never get any better than this, I just thought, 'Oh, he'll never be able to raise his arm again', and I was quite pleased at that thought. Does that sound awful?

Of course, he takes a lot of looking after, I have to do everything for him now. He was only 54 when it happened, six years ago. He was a different man then. He was so active, always doing something, I never knew what. He worked in the Electricity Board, they say he was good at his job and the life and soul of the office. They called him Collie and he went to all the staff dinners and outings, though I was never asked.

The first thing I did after his stroke was to learn to drive, so I could take him out a bit. I've got one of those adapted cars, with a hoist thingy for his wheelchair, but I just can't get the hang of it. I usually go to some nice viewpoint and park, I love a nice view. The special seat in the car is so difficult for me to turn, though, so poor Colin is facing the wrong way – but at least he's out of the house, isn't he? I go for a little walk, or if there's a cafe nearby, I have a coffee. I don't think he minds waiting, it's hard to tell, but I've noticed that he seems to get cold quite quickly. Oh well.

It's a pity he can't feed himself, it must be so humiliating being spoon-fed. I play little games with him, to make it fun. I bring the spoon slowly near his mouth, singing a silly song about trains and tunnels, then just when he's about to get it, I snatch it away! Train cancelled! We do have a laugh at that – well I do, anyway. I'm convinced it's helping his reflexes, too. If the food gets cold I still make sure he finishes it all, – especially if it's spicy, he was never keen on spicy food, but it must stimulate the palate, don't you think? It's amazing how he eats curry now, whereas before the stroke, he would have thrown it in the bin and I must confess, he would swear most fluently.

Television's a great thing if you're housebound, isn't it? Colin loved television, especially football, he watched it all the time. That is, when he wasn't watching those programmes full of naughty ladies, after I'd gone to bed. Oh dear, how he hated the soaps, and all that, I never got to see any. Of course, it's different now, and I think it's bad for his health to watch football, he might get too excited if someone scores a goal. And it certainly would be too exciting for him to see those naughty ladies, though I don't think they're all that ladylike. Now it's Emmerdale, Coronation Street, Holly-whats-its-name and all the rest, and I'm sure he's glad for me to see them, because I'm taking such good care of him. I push his chair up close to the television and turn up the sound, so he dosen't miss anything.

Holidays were something he loved, he planned every detail, got the cheapest deals, he was good at that. He didn't like flying so we never went abroad, we just went south, or once, to Scotland. I'll never forget our last holiday, when we toured the coastal route in the west. He was a very keen photographer, very pernickety about composing a snap – or a 'shot' as he called it. Landscapes were his favourite, but sometimes he needed a person included to give it perspective, I suppose. I'm sure it was my fault, because I never seemed to get it right, but then I'm not artistic, so he'd have to shout at me,

"Left a bit – no, not that much! Left, I said, left, you stupid cow!"

And so on. And on.

Well, on that holiday, there was a pretty little bridge just before a quaint village, over a fairly fast flowing river, and of course he needed to take a photograph. With a figure in it, to balance it, he said. There was I, trying to do what he wanted, and there was he, yelling at me, going purple in the face with frustration – I'm sure it was my fault, and he didn't mean to call me all those names.

He was backing away, yelling,

"Turn your head around, as if you're looking at something on the other side – go on, a bit more, I don't want your stupid face in it."

He was so engrossed in taking the perfect shot that he backed towards the river without noticing. I opened my mouth to warn him, but he snarled,

"I said look away, you lump of lard – and keep your mouth shut."

So I said nothing, and he backed right over the bank into the river.

I couldn't believe it. He didn't reappear. He was gone. I waited about fifteen minutes or so, to make sure, then just as I was thinking I'd stroll into the village to report it, a man who was fishing further downstream started calling for help.

Colin was very lucky. He was unconscious when they pulled him out, but the paramedics revived him. Of course, in such a rural area, there was a long wait for the ambulance, they say that's why he had the stroke on the way to the hospital.

After that, I tore up all his photographs and burnt them, because I don't want him to get upset that he can't take photos anymore, never mind go on holiday. I quite like flying, so I go abroad twice a year. Colin goes into a Care Home when I'm away. It's not an especially nice one, but Colin did love a bargain.

I try to make life interesting for him, go different places, do different things. We often go to that shopping mall near the big roundabout, it's quite handy to where we live. He never liked shopping so I leave the car in a corner of the car park, where he can 'people watch', isn't that what they call it? I don't take him into the shops, it would be too much for him. Sometimes I'm away four or five hours, it's such a big place.

I think it's very important to give him every chance to be as healthy as possible. There isn't a treatment nor therapy that I don't know of. I give him vitamin injections regularly, though I'm not very good with the needle. I give him cold baths to keep his blood moving, at least I think that's what it does. Exercise is very important too, and I stretch his legs and arms as far as I can get them to go, to keep him supple. He's so grateful to me, often there's tears in his eyes.

I'm a great believer in traditional medicine, so I put hot mustard compresses on his chest – I actually don't know how effective they are, and they do tend to rip some skin off when I remove them, but I wouldn't want Colin to miss out on anything.

Yes, I make sure that Colin gets exactly what he deserves.

Oh, is that the time? It's been lovely to talk to you, but I must fly.

Enema time!

THE ETIQUETTE OF BURGLARY

GEORGE AND PATRICK

The Eighteenth of March.

George awoke, as often before, to a musty, gritty feeling like soil in his mouth, a stench of vomit, and a thunderous headache. His face was pressed into soft wet grass, his clothes pungently damp.

"Fuck it!"

He rolled onto his back, to find himself staring into a thick, cloying early morning mist and an unnerving feeling of nothingness around and below him.

He had no idea where he was.

"What the fuck.......?"

He lay still for a few minutes, then gingerly sat up, his head reeling, wishing the ground beneath him would stop spinning.

Staggering to his feet, he swayed unsteadily, peering into the mist. He had an uneasy feeling that someone was watching him, and fancied he saw a tall shadowy figure looming above him.

"What the fuck are ye lookin' at? Fuck off!"

His words disappeared into the silent whiteness. He sat down heavily, his legs having had enough, his thoughts a wild jumble of cheering and jeering, crowds pushing and shoving, raised glasses, empty glasses, shamrocks, green hats, arguments, leading a parade........did he lead a parade? No, he tried to lead a parade, but those bastards manhandled him out of his moment of glory, didn't they, the scum........ A wave of nausea washed over him, and he vomited copiously.

"Shit! It's fuckin' all over me!"

"Well, you shouldn't have drunk so much, should you?" said a disembodied voice.

George stared wildly around. The mist had retreated a little, but he could see no-one there at all, nothing except a huge stone statue of Saint Patrick.

"Who said that? Who's there?"

With some difficulty, George got to his feet. He crept all the way around the base of the statue, clinging to the metal fence that surrounded it. There was nobody there. He looked around as the mist evaporated, the landscape unfolding before him, and gave a great shout of relief,

"I know where I am! I'm at fuckin' Slieve Patrick! How the fuck did I get here?"

"Mind your language, George!"

The voice sounded again, and George, totally sober now, felt the hairs prickle up the back of his neck.

"Who……..? ..How?…………how did I get here?"

"Oh it's a long story, George, but I was watching you – all the way."

"W…Watchin' me? Where….where are you?"

He looked intently at the impassive face of the huge stone figure looming above him. The stone surface seemed to shift imperceptibly, as though the stone particles had become fluid., and George said in wonder,

"It's you talkin', isn't it? You up there – Patrick!"

"Yes, it's me," came the cold, contemptuous voice again. "You are a complete drunkard, a wife-beater, a. ….."

Here George interrupted peevishly,

"Now look here, ye fuckin' statue, I'm no drunk – everyone has a few too many sometimes – and that bitch of a wife of mine left last week, so I can't be beatin' her now, can I?".

"Don't interrupt" said the voice, as sharply as stone could speak. "Yesterday, you nearly ruined my parade, prancing about the street, shouting obscenities, pushing the man representing me aside, – not to mention threatening the stewards with a crozier!

"Well, I'm as good as anyone to lead the parade," said George in a sulky tone, "sure that ejit wasn't even from Downpatrick."

"No, he wasn't," the voice agreed, "but at least he was sober!"

"I could lead the fuckin' parade, at least I'm from the town," George swore some more, just for good measure, but the voice sounded loudly,

"Watch your language, George! You're a foul-mouthed drunk, and always will be!".

"Oh, high and mighty now, aren't you?" sneered George. "I bet I could fuckin' sober up any fuckin' time I want – "

"You could not!"

"Yes I fuckin' could!"

"Couldn't!"

"Could!"

"Could not!".

Thoroughly muddled by their verbal sparring, George and Patrick fell silent. George shivered, wrapping his arms around himself, stamping his feet to restore some circulation. 'How does he talk without movin' his lips?' he wondered, ' I bet I could lead that bloody parade!'.

As though he had spoken out loud, the voice replied,

"Well, since you've mentioned bets, here's a proposition for you. I'll bet that you can't stay sober and keep a clean tongue in your head for a whole year. If you can, I'll speak to you on this day next year, in front of whoever you bring to hear me. Then you'll be a celebrity, and your wife will forgive you and come home. Oh, and you must lead next year's parade. Sober."

"Do I have to take the wife back?" asked George.

"That's optional!".

Relieved, George slyly ventured,

"What if I just tell people now? And you can stuff your poxy bet!".

"You are a drunkard, George! Nobody will believe you!".

"Alright, alright – I'll think about it".

Gazing out over Strangford Lough, George thought he had nothing to lose, anyway. Even his drinking pals had quickly deserted him when things got a bit rough, and he knew this was his last chance to be the 'Somebody' he was convinced he could be.

"Throw in a lift back to the town, and it's a deal!".

George had never, ever, attempted to stop drinking, but he was determined to win his bet. After a couple of days trying to abstain, he was almost sick with longing for alcohol, any kind of alcohol, and on the brink of succumbing. So, after years of denying that he had a drink problem, he almost fell in through the door where the Alcoholic's Anonymous meetings were held. His short period of abstinence had knocked all the fight out of George. Unaware that he was not only filthy, but also extremely smelly, George sat down meekly, afraid to speak in case he inadvertently swore. It was going to be a long year.

'Keeping a clean tongue in my head – how hard can it be?', thought George, but changing the unconscious habit of a lifetime proved to be almost impossible. He found that the best way to ensure he didn't swear was to say as little as possible. He found himself forced to listen to other people, instead of shouting them down in his former belligerent way, and gradually, a new George began to emerge.

The Twelfth of July celebrations, the Viking Festival, Fireworks displays, Christmas and New Year all passed by, and George managed to survive somehow. He discovered that when he was sober and quiet, he became acceptable at last, and as he had never been taken seriously before, he began to think there was something in this tee-total thing after all.

In early February, George presented himself at the reception desk in the local Council Office.

"I want to put me name forward for Saint Patrick!" he declared, putting a crumpled entry form before a startled receptionist. Gingerly, she lifted the grubby sheet of paper, dropping it onto a pile, with a disinterested ' Okay'. All he could do now was wait.

In due course, the choice was made – and George was selected. He was not surprised, but accepted the honour as though it were his due.

'I'm home and dry!' he thought gleefully, laughing at his own witty pun, a surge of self-importance restoring his somewhat dented confidence. As the great day approached, George became increasingly bombastic, and the organisers became increasingly anxious. He was at pains to declare to anyone who would listen that he was now 'stone cold sober!', then he would break into uproarious laughter, vastly amused by some secret joke. His nomination had only been the result of internal wrangling which had backfired, and George was not to know that they had a stand-in, in case George was unfit.

On the morning of the parade, he woke early, and donned the costume of Saint Patrick. He regarded himself in the mirror, and gave a salute of approval to his image. He didn't know which he was looking forward to most – showing that statue he was as good as the next man to lead his parade, or that long, long pint he had promised himself all through the past dry year. The parade wasn't due to start for several hours, but George wanted to get full mileage from this day, so he sallied forth, swaggering into the town centre, checking his reflection in every shop window as he passed.

"Yer lookin' great!" "Can the child have her photo with ye'? "Is that a real beard?" "Do you want a pint?" "A burger?" "Are your feet not freezin' in them sandals?"

People stopped to shake his hand, or pose for a photograph, their arm draped round him as though they were friends. George loved every moment. The only time that he had been the centre of attention previously had been when he was involved in a fight, or was being ejected from a pub, or appearing in court – occasions when he was regarded as a complete waste of time. Now, he basked in this new feeling of being included and wanted.

Striding down through the crowds thronging Market street, he saw crates of beer being unloaded outside his former favourite bar, and smiled broadly to himself, intending to sweep on by.

"Oh! My back! Arghhh....!"

"What's that you said?" George swung round, an ugly expression on his face, but seeing the delivery man bent over in obvious distress, he stopped, saying grandly,

"Don't move, I'll carry them – I know where the cellar is."

Grabbing a heavy crate, he managed to load it on to a trolley, and soon had four crates ready to wheel to the cellar. His first flush of enthusiasm for the task waned as he pushed it along, shouting at the barman as he passed through,

"Your deliveryman's banjaxed his back – I think he needs a doctor!"

Breathing heavily, he got to the cellar door, and leaned the trolley against the wall. 'I'm not liftin' them again' he decided, 'I'll get out the back door – they can lift their own beer!'.

Hastily he pushed his way out through the security door, being well acquainted with it's location, but he skidded on a greasy mix of spilt beer and old cooking oil, landing heavily on his side.

"F....for flip's sake! Me coat!"

He hauled himself upright, and inspected the damage. His coat had a long, oily smear on the side, in addition to a torn sleeve, and the knee was ripped in his trousers, blood dripping from a cut down his leg. Something was dripping from the torn sleeve, too, and he sniffed it........ yes, it was beer. His hat was crushed out of shape, and his new found love for his fellow man had disappeared.

"Shi......sugar! I'll have to get cleaned up before the parade! That's what I get for helpin' them bas...barmen!"

Pausing only to tidy himself as best he could, he hurried back onto Market street, deciding the chemist would help him. Bursting in through the door, his hair awry, looking as though he'd been fighting, he pushed his way in front of others waiting to be served, demanding instant attention. The chemist was used to patching him up from time to time, so he calmly tended to the cuts as best he could, resolving let the organisers of the parade know that the stand-in should be ready. That the stand-in was himself had no bearing on his decision. None at all. Obviously.

Rushing out of the shop, George realised that his torn clothing was flapping about, and so he crossed the road and went into the library. Reaching over the front of the desk, he lifted a stapler, and proceeded to mend the tears and rips in his costume. The librarian, knowing from past experience that it was never wise to provoke George, merely rolled her eyes and turned back to chatting on the telephone, letting him get on with it.

****

"Well, here I am!"

George presented himself to the stewards at the assembly point, an anxious eagerness in his voice. He knew that he looked a little ragged, but surely they would overlook a rip or two. Accustomed as he was to the smell of stale beer, George didn't realise that the aroma of the beer he had fallen into clung to his clothes, giving him every appearance of being drunk. People milled about, making last-minute adjustments to their floats, putting costumes on, blowing up balloons. Amongst the throng, a group of officials huddled together, talking urgently, then one of them approached George.

"Well now, George, how are you?"

"Grand, just grand." George answered tightly, not liking the man's tone.

"So, you're good then, George, are you?"

"I am that!".

The conversation reached stalemate, and the official glanced over his shoulder at his colleagues in a mute appeal for support.

"Well now," he began, "It's like this George, you see the thing is, well, the fact is…."

"What the fu….what are ye tryin' to say?" said George, pushing his face menacingly close, "C'mon, spit it out!"

"Well, this is a community parade, and there's wee children here, and all the clergymen……we can't be having drink, or anyone with drink on them, in the middle of it, especially Saint Patrick!".

"Whaaat?" Are you telling me I'm drunk?" Roaring like a bull, George swung his fist at the man, who nimbly dodged behind the others, one of whom unwisely observed,

"Sure we can smell the drink off you from here!".

All the suppressed angry tensions of the past year exploded in George's brain, and he launched himself at the man, fists flailing wildly. There was a brief scuffle, then the all too familiar scenario of the police van, the strong grip hauling him into the cell, the door locking and the steady voice of the policeman assuring George that he'd get out tomorrow when he had sobered up.

****

Next morning, a beaten George walked down Irish Street, with the intention of getting mightily, spectacularly drunk. Suddenly, he stopped dead on the pavement.

'Hold on a minute, I never said a single bad word yesterday, did I? And I did lead the parade – it's just that I was in a police van! But it went down the street first, didn't it? It's today that yer man's going to speak, it's today! All I need now is a few witnesses!'

Immensely cheered by this reasoning, he went about the business of gathering up some people to see the miracle. He had plenty of drinking pals, but they were all sleeping off the excesses of yesterday, and were disinclined to follow another of George's crazy schemes. He tried the parish priest, the Presbyterian minister, the Methodist pastor, but without success. By now, he had a vicious headache as his stress levels rose. The town was quiet, many of the shops closed, and he looked for somewhere to buy some painkillers. As he passed the chemist's shop, he saw the owner inside, preparing to lock up. He tried the door, and it duly opened.

"Have ye anything for a headache?"

The chemist thought George was about to tackle him for taking his place yesterday, and looked around for an escape route, but no, George only needed painkillers. Relieved, the chemist brought George a glass of water, gave him some aspirin, and offered to drive him home.

"Tell ye what, I want to get out to Slieve Patrick, ye can run me out there!"

****

George and the chemist toiled up the steep hill towards the summit of Slieve Patrick. The grass was damp and they slithered and slipped, holding onto each other. A low-lying mist obscured the top, the road below them disappeared, and the chemist felt he was living out some surreal punishment for yesterday. At last, they staggered up the final few yards, George letting go of the chemist so suddenly that he fell on his knees, his smart trousers grinding into the soft mud.

A long, high-pitched wailing sounded, and the chemist looked up, to see George wringing his hands in despair, staring in disbelief at the devastation around him. The protective fence had been broken, twisted metal like swords pointing skywards. Saint Patrick had been toppled over, with chips of stone scattered about, and one hand missing, lying full length with his face towards the sky. Beer cans and bottles littered the ground, and George, heartbroken, wailed louder, raging against the sight. The chemist was alarmed at the depth of George's grief, and as he continued to mourn noisily and despairingly, the chemist found himself patting him on the back, making comforting sounds, as though George were a child.

Just when the chemist was beginning to fear for George's mental state, and was considering calling for help, George abruptly stopped.

"Well, Patrick, I kept my word!" he said in a controlled, almost dignified manner, "I haven't had a drink for a whole year, and not one curse went past my lips. And I did get picked to lead the parade – even if it was in a police van!".

Then George's voice lifted, and he roared belligerently at the fallen statue.

"And all the time, you bastard, you were up here drinkin' and pissin' yourself and fallin' over! Have ye nothin' to say for yourself?"

No sound issued from the set, stone lips.

"Well, fuck you anyway!"

Aiming a kick at Saint Patrick's head, George spied the chemist looking on in astonishment.

"What are you lookin' at? Fuck off!"

Then delivering another kick that crunched his toes painfully, George limped off down the slope, his words trailing behind him like a banner,

"He's not even fuckin' from Downpatrick!",

while a gentle hiccup sounded soft on the air behind him.

AFTERNOON TEA

Alicia simply couldn't remember which of the cupcakes she had put the arsenic on. Most confusing. She peered closely at the pretty cakes, on the top tier of her Royal Doulton cake-stand, above the lower tier of neatly cut cucumber sandwiches.

There was the one with pink icing, a cherry sitting on top, which Alicia knew Miss Wilson would choose. Next to it, a rather violently coloured yellow lemon-flavoured one, destined for the sour lips of the Vicar. White icing, smothered in multi-coloured vermicelli would be the choice of uncouth George Lane, her solicitor. Her nephew Brian, with his plump face and girlish manner, would choose the thick, sticky chocolate confection.

It was the first Tuesday of the month, when Alicia held afternoon tea at three o'clock exactly. It was a firmly established ritual, and Alicia knew her guest's preferences with certainty. It was always the same company, over whom Alicia fancied she held not a little power, each having 'expectations' of varying amounts, when in the distant future her estate would be distributed.

It was two-thirty, and Alicia sighed at the prospect of waiting. She was a little hungry. Looking admiringly at the small, low table, beautifully set with china on a snow-white linen cloth, the cake-stand a genteel centrepiece, she stared closely at the cakes again. The sugar she had sprinkled over each one glistened invitingly, and she quite forgot about the arsenic. Lately, she had been forgetting rather a lot. She settled herself comfortably in the wide leather armchair, and leaning back, closed her eyes, thinking a little doze would be nice, before her guests arrived. As she drifted pleasantly into a light slumber, images of the expected guests slowly unfurled behind her closed eyelids.

Miss Wilson irritated Alicia beyond endurance, with her simpering manner, her ridiculous high-pitched laugh, her long yellow teeth. Those decaying molars reminded Alicia of a cat. A very old cat. A very old family cat, of which her sister Bronwyn had been particularly fond. What was it's name? Busby? No, not that...Bushy, perhaps? Anyhow, it didn't matter what it was called, Bronwyn was besotted by it since she had been given it for her sixth birthday. Alicia hated that cat, and as it aged, it became smelly and occasionally flea-ridden. Bronwyn insisted on bringing it into the house, and sometimes, it could be found curled up on a bed, purring throatily. The day Alicia found it on her bed, retching mightily as it brought up a furball on her pillow, was the cat's last day on earth. She gathered it up roughly, and sped quietly down the stairs, ignoring it's painful heaving. In the tackroom over the stables, she found the crystalline substance the gardener used for killing rats. Uncertain as she was as to how to administer the poison, there was a brief stay of execution for the cat, but observant Alicia soon worked out just what to do, and Busby? Bushy?… was no more.

Miss Wilson, who was not much younger than Alicia, showed her great yellow teeth and mottled gums when she laughed, or spoke, or ate. Alicia hated her for that, as well as the robust health that made her suppose she would outlive Alicia. She hated her quite as much as she had hated Bronwyn's cat.

Stirring in her chair, Alicia's eyelids fluttered open briefly. The October wind whisked dry autumn leaves against the window, scratching and rattling impatiently. In the quiet room, the fire glowed bright, the clock ticked steadily. It was twenty minutes to three.

Peacefully, Alicia dozed again. The Vicar's dour face had never inspired her, his long doleful sermons had never prompted her to seek salvation, nor moved her to repentance. His arrogant assumption that she would bequeath a significant sum to church funds amused her, and she was aware that he attended these occasions only to secure such a promise. It gave Alicia considerable entertainment to toy with him. She would ponder aloud the merits of other worthy causes, beg for his advice, and than watch gleefully as he tried to deflect her interest in foreign orphanages, donkey sanctuaries or missionaries in China. No, these things did not bother her at all, she knew she held the whip hand. However, what did raise her temper to impotent fury was the irrefutable certainty that she could not take her fortune with her, and the Vicar very unwisely frequently advised her of that fact, intoning ponderously, 'There are no pockets in a shroud', every time he saw an opportunity. If only he knew how deeply Alicia resented this, how she railed against a God who would prise her fingers from her possessions, from her money. Her money! Alicia did not want to leave it to anyone, she wanted to take it with her, but the Vicar's very presence told her she was powerless, she could not thwart God.

How sweet it would be to see that mean tight mouth open wide in a rictus of agony, those sour lips stretched until they were bloodily torn across his gums!

A shower of sparks leapt up the chimney as the logs settled in the grate. The clock gave a single solemn note to mark the last quarter of an hour before three o'clock, but Alicia did not hear it. So much of life seemed to be half-dreamed lately, and Alicia often found herself unable to separate waking from sleeping, present from past. Her thoughts drifted aimlessly, until they settled again at last. She saw clearly the hard countenance of George Lane, heard his hectoring voice, breathed in the scent of his nauseating aftershave. She would not have chosen such a man to act for her, but when her own family solicitor had retired, George, as the junior partner, had taken over. So far, Alicia had not managed to move her business elsewhere. He had taken to calling unexpectedly, his eyes darting around as he rudely entered her house without asking, as though in a covert assessment of her possessions. She fancied his presence brought an undertone of menace and she tried to remain alert whenever he called. Sometimes, she jerked awake in her chair, to find him sitting uncomfortably close, staring hard at her. She was disturbed by these occasional lapses of clarity, and would cover up as best she could, frostily dismissing him, but quite unable to recall how long he had been there, or what their conversation had been. She carried a recent hazy memory of a stronger, cruel hand clasping hers, a pen being roughly forced between her fingers, but she could not tell whether it had really happened, or it was just a nasty dream.

Her lips trembled a little, betraying disquieting weakness. Suddenly, a clear picture of George Lane's large hand came to her, closing round a colourful cupcake. She saw him raise it to his mouth, saw his teeth crunching down through the sweet, sugary icing with relish. She tittered maliciously. George Lane would never lay a finger on a penny of her money.

Opening one rheumy eye, Alicia noted there remained ten minutes before three on the clock, so she allowed herself to slip easily into shallow sleep once more. Now Thomas Larkin's handsome face smiled at her, hazel eyes laughing. She hadn't thought of him in years, not since she had fallen passionately in love with him, but he had married her younger sister, Bronwyn, instead. Then she hated him.

She had really only meant to make him a little sick. As he groomed Bronwyn's ancient pony one cold February morning, some four months after their wedding, Alicia came into the stable. Sweetly, she offered him a warming cup of hot tea, carefully stirring in the sugar from the tin in the gardener's cupboard. No-one saw her as she made her way back to the house through the shrubbery, and she was quietly reading in the study when the body was discovered. It was generally thought to be a tragedy, a dreadful accident! So easy to mistake one substance for the other! It was admitted that Thomas had not been familiar with the gardener's habits, but of course the man was sacked at once.

At the funeral, Bronwyn's grief was noisy and prolonged, her loud wails drowning out the muted tones of those gathered at Thomas' burial. Alicia was disgusted at such unseemly behaviour, and when Bronwyn, prostrating herself across the coffin, was copiously sick, Alicia had nothing but contempt for a man who could choose a simpleton like her sister, instead of her. The mourners walked slowly from the graveyard, and Alicia considered the episode satisfactorily closed.

But not quite! Bronwyn's continuing sickness each morning told another story, and in a few short months, Alicia was a distinctly unenthusiastic aunt. He was named Brian, after his maternal grandfather. As the child grew, he held no hint of his father in his looks. He possessed his mother's fine, flyaway brown hair, her pink soft skin which reddened all too easily, and full wet lips. He also had her myopic, staring brown eyes, and faintly anxious air. Alicia was not beguiled by his baby ways, and seldom noticed him, nor acknowledged him. Inexplicably, he loved his severe aunt completely, and squealed with unbridled delight whenever he saw her. He crawled at her feet, clinging to her skirts while she tried to shoo him away. He brought her childish presents of pine cones from the garden, or bunches of wild flowers from the meadow, clutched in his sticky little hands. He even shyly brought his first school report to her, blushing furiously at her off-hand praise. When Bronwyn married for the second time, he was heart-broken, as it meant he had to move some distance away. Each summer, he spent a long holiday with his beloved aunt, and cried sorely when it was time to leave. Alicia could not understand it, for she never encouraged him in the least. Now, he still loved his cantankerous aunt. He worried about her welfare, calling regularly to make sure she wanted for nothing. His love was genuine, and he neither wanted or needed anything from her. Though Alicia could tolerate his devoted care without undue dislike, he was her still despised, unforgiven sister's son. And he was Thomas Larkin's child.

The fire burned low, and Alicia awoke, slightly chilled, just as the clock struck three. She surveyed the room vacantly for a moment, before her gaze settled on the table. Where were her guests? A small measure of anger began to grow in her, for she was accustomed to punctuality. Pulling a rug around her knees, she decided not to put any more logs on the fire. Let them freeze as punishment! The clock ticked more loudly, it seemed, and as the seconds and minutes went by, Alicia's anger grew to dull rage. She was cold..... and hungry. She reached towards the cupcakes, and selected Miss Wilson's pink one. Something made her hesitate as she lifted it to her mouth, but then she ate it greedily, crumbs scattering around her. She was still hungry, so the Vicar's lemon cupcake disappeared next, followed swiftly by George Lane's vermicelli-coated one. It seemed silly to leave the last cupcake alone on the plate, so she crammed the one destined for her nephew greedily into her mouth, smearing chocolate on her chin as she gobbled like a querulous old turkey.

Alicia lay back in her chair, feeling vaguely uneasy. Her gaze travelled around the room, until it fell on the desk calendar, near her chair. The room had dimmed about her, but Alicia could see the word 'Monday' quite clearly, just as she remembered which of the cupcakes she had put the arsenic on.

She had sprinkled it liberally, lovingly......on all of them!

A LITTLE TASTER

It was deathly cold in the Great Hall. The old king gathered his musty robes around his skinny mottled limbs, and moved closer to the meagre fire. Slowly, slowly, he turned his malevolent gaze to the right, his eyes glittering like tiny spiteful shards of glass.

Shivering in the bone-chilling cold, a line of seven children stood quietly, six boys and one girl. They were waiting for the moment when the king would choose one of them at random to taste his food before he ate. They were all children of his various retainers, including the cook who was preparing his meal at the end of the gloomy room. The king trusted no-one.

The cook calmly went about his business, chopping, stirring, slicing. Life under the old king was intolerable. Cruelty, fear, poverty, hunger, – it could not go on like this. Secret meetings were held, whispered words barely uttered, breathless decisions made. Someone must act, sacrifices must be made.

The cook shook his sleeve lightly as he stirred the pot, and the powder slid silently into the mix. The slow acting poison would not commence its work for some hours, but then it would be certain death for anyone who had eaten even the smallest piece of the stew bubbling on the cooking fire.

Out of the corner of his eye, he caught a covert glimpse of the flame red tendrils of his beloved daughter's hair, framing her innocent face, as she waited in line for the king to make his choice. She had been chosen the previous night, and the cook was almost confident that the king would overlook her tonight.

The king rose to his feet. The cook began to ladle the aromatic, deadly stew into a bowl, his back to the king. Stretching out his arm, the king pointed, his blackened, filthy nail tracing a slow line along the waiting child tasters. There wasn't a sound. The air seemed to still, as the cruel hand stopped.

The cook turned around, and his eyes widened in horror as he watched his daughter advance trustingly towards him, her tiny hand outstretched for the bowl.

PICK IT UP AND RUN WITH IT

Jack knew he was going mad. As he allowed that thought to finally lodge in the scrambled mess that was his consciousness, another string of meaningless phrases began to trawl across his mind, like endless ticker – tape passing over his brain, then reflecting into the back of his eyes.

"Pick it up and run with it!" screamed a random sentence from the endless litany in his head, another following on it's heels, crying "I hate you!", "I hate you!", "Twenty black horses!", "Order! Order!", "Do unto others..."

Sweat oozed from his every pore, slithering into his eyes, stinging and blinding as he drove towards the Armagh roundabout on his way to work. This had been going on for weeks now, and Jack didn't know how much longer he could go on. He began to chant each disconnected thought as it appeared, in a high, fraught childish tone – "Be a good boy, now!"- "A big bottle of water"-"Carry me, Daddy, carry me!"- "I'm going now, I don't know where's the exit?"- "I hate you!" – "it's teabags again!" – Oh! Pick it up and run with it! Pick it up and run with it!"

For a brief second, his vision cleared and he realised he was at the roundabout junction. The car in front, waiting to ease out into the traffic, loomed up with sickening speed, and he froze, unable to brake as he shot forward. The grinding of metal, the screech of brakes, the impact of his body against the steering wheel, drove all the breath out of his lungs. For a few wondrous seconds, there was complete silence. Slumped across the front seat, he could hear his own breathing, shallow and fast, the faint ticking noise of some part of the engine, the soft sighing hiss of water leaking from the radiator onto warm metal. There was no sound in his brain. It was a moment of pure bliss.

Then the world, and the words, cranked up again, and as the firemen were cutting him free from the wreckage, he could be heard mumbling, "Pick it up and run with it!" "Pick it up and run with it!"

The paramedics in the ambulance questioned him gently, asking for phone numbers, his wife's name, any medical conditions, but he made no attempt to reply. He held himself rigid, feeling no pain, although blood trickled from his forehead and his ankle was twisted into a grotesque shape. Inside his head, the words swirled and whispered endlessly. As he lay on a trolley in a casualty area, noise rose up all around him. Voices spoke over him, people bumped into the trolley, doors banged, phones shrilled.

At last, a doctor arrived. He examined Jack, probing and poking, making little comments to himself as he worked. He turned to a nurse who had been hovering at his side, and ordered peremptorily that Jack's ankle be x-rayed, his forehead stitched. Then, with a condescending half-smile, told Jack that he would be just fine, no danger or serious damage, just a straightforward break. Without waiting for a reply, he strode off down the corridor, barking orders and criticisms in equal measure. Jack stared after him like a child who was being abandoned, for as soon as the doctor departed, the questions began again. A girl in a blue uniform began to talk gently to him, asking did he require any pain relief. He shook his head dumbly. Then she enquired about his family – who should come for him when his injures were treated, as he would be able to go home then. Awkwardly, he turned slightly on the trolley, and pulled out his wallet. He handed it to the girl, who took it to the nearby desk, and he could see his driving license being examined, along with other personal documents. Presently, she came back to him, and sat on the edge of the trolley.

"You're going down to have your ankle set," she said, taking his hand in hers, and patting it comfortingly. "Now, don't worry about your stitches, because I'm going to do them now before that, and I promise I won't hurt you!" She turned to lift the necessary tools, saying over her shoulder, "Oh! and we've got in touch with your wife, she's on her way."

That was when Jack realised there was no escape.

Sheila swept into the hospital, through the swinging doors which quivered with her passing, exasperation imbued in her every movement. Having ascertained on the telephone that Jack's injuries were not life-threatening, she was by now thoroughly irritated by the inconvenience of his carelessness, and the necessity of having to leave a Very Important Meeting at the school where she worked to collect him. At the Reception desk, she demanded to be taken to him at once, and as was usual with Sheila, someone complied quickly with her demand. In a small side ward, Jack heard her approach with resignation, her rich, full voice rising effortlessly above the hospital din.

"There you are!" she intoned, disapproval in every syllable. "What on earth have you done this time?" and Jack felt, as always, like a small boy caught in a particularly nasty misdemeanour. Before a reply could be given, a nurse arrived to offer a wheelchair and crutches, to be returned when no longer needed. Sheila, deciding any input from Jack would be superfluous, opted for the crutches only, shuddering slightly at the thought of a wheelchair scraping her perfectly decorated walls. She kept up a stream of questions, comments and admonishments as she drove them both home, while Jack lay back against the headrest, trying to sort the words in his head from those issuing from his wife's mouth. He managed the transfer from car to front door, pausing on the step to take a long shuddering breath, before finally gaining the soft sanctum of the downstairs guest bedroom.

He sank into the deep mattress, and closed his eyes while Sheila continued her monologue, in and out of the room, lifting cushions, moving chairs, asking questions.

"This won't do for more than a night or two" she said, leaning against the door and surveying him critically. "I don't want this room messed up, and anyway, a soft mattress is no good for your back. Jack! Are you listening?" Lying still, breathing slowly, Jack appeared to be asleep. Sheila waited for a moment, then with a small sigh of relief, left the room, closing the door behind her. She moved about the house, making a hasty dinner, showering, making phone calls, watching television. Occasionally, she went to check on Jack, but he pretended to be asleep, until at last, she went upstairs to bed, and the house fell silent.

Jack lay as still as possible, hoping that if his body was quiet, perhaps his mind might also be still. He tried to think louder than the jumbled words that tormented him, imagining the sounds of the various drills he used in the dental surgery. He tried to isolate each individual pitch, and for a while, it seemed to work, the buzz of the tiny fine drill to the deep growl of the heavy one, but then he began to hear the ragged breathing of his patients, the guttural sound of the suction tube, and he found himself repeating over and over, in a sibilant whisper, "No fillings, silly bitch, no fillings!" Towards dawn, he spiralled down into uneasy sleep, the words gathered like malevolent gremlins in a corner of his subconscious.

"Jack! Wake up!"

Sheila's cutting voice brought Jack back to unwilling wakefulness. "It's like being smacked across the face with my own name" he thought, as he struggled to rise to the surface of morning lethargy.

"The police are here – they want to interview you about yesterday". She looked distastefully at his dishevelled state, as he had slept in the clothes he was wearing, too exhausted to undress the night before.

"Come along, they're in the study", so Jack obediently followed Sheila into the small tidy room where no-one ever studied. He glanced at his watch and was startled to find it was almost eleven o'clock, and silently offered a prayer of thankfulness for having slept at last. Two policemen sat in the room and Jack felt like bursting into laughter, thinking that it was rather like an absurd B – movie interrogation scene. He smiled idiotically at them, but failed to hear them speaking, as in his head a single phrase kept going round and round. "Captain Cook and the Jolly Roger! Captain Cook and the Jolly... what was it?" At last, he realised that they were looking at him expectantly, and it dawned on him that some response was needed. Finding that he couldn't marshal his thoughts sufficiently to produce a reply, he simply sat, staring back at them, afraid to speak in case he blurted out something stupid.

With great patience, the policemen tried to encourage Jack to speak, even enlisting Sheila's help, but to no avail. Jack simply could not speak.

"He was fine yesterday, not like this...." began Sheila, but then it dawned on her that, actually, Jack had not spoken at all since the accident, not a single word. She beckoned the policemen out of the room, and Jack heard the steady murmur of their voices in the hall, then the door closing behind them, and Sheila's snapping footsteps coming back towards the study.

She gazed at him for a moment, as though he were a puzzle she must unravel, then said decisively, "This is ridiculous, Jack, just ridiculous." She tried for a short while to elicit a response of any sort from him, but finally said, "O.K. You think this is a game, don't you? Well, I'm not putting up with it, you're going back to the hospital – right now".

Three hours later, they left the hospital together, Jack mute, Sheila ranting ceaselessly as she drove. "Post traumatic stress... is that all they can come up with?" She enumerated all the problems that they would have, from Jack having to get a locum in the surgery, to not being able to socialise, communicate by phone and, worst of all, not knowing how long it would last. Glancing at Jack, she realised that he was smiling. In his head, a pleasant mantra had taken hold and for once, he welcomed the words wheeling around. "Off to the Galway races," he thought happily, "Off to the Galway races!"

For a few days, Jack pottered about contentedly during the day, managing to move around without too much trouble on his crutches. The ever present cacophony of words and phrases clamouring for expression faded into the background, and he began to think a little more coherently. He sang snatches of songs under his breath, as though it would wake someone if he sang out loud. He turned off all the appliances that made any sound, including the fridge, to Sheila's annoyance, and made no attempt to speak at all when she came home. But he knew that this state of affairs would soon stop, when the summer holidays for all schools began, and Sheila would be home all day, every day. Gradually, his feelings of well – being left him, ebbing away under the constant knowledge that he must begin to live in the real world again, sooner rather than later. His thoughts became disjointed again, and he barely succeeded in concealing the turmoil inside him. The slightest sounds disturbed him profoundly, and he yearned for total silence. Peace and quiet.

Once, when Sheila was gone to work, he made his way as far as the main road nearby. He kept close to the hedges and fences along the way, wary of falling, or worse still, meeting someone he knew. When he reached the main road, he moved jerkily on his crutches, dangerously close to the traffic, not knowing why he had come here. He suddenly remembered, with piercing clarity, the blessed silence after the crash, and he turned without warning onto the road, into the path of an oncoming car. Brakes screamed, he had a glimpse of a young woman's look of horror, as she swerved away from him, horns blared, drivers gestured angrily. The car had missed him, but he knew with despairing certainty that he could have caused someone to be killed. Shakily, he regained the pavement, and made his way back to the house. That evening, Sheila's endless voice lodged deeper than ever in his brain and tortured him all night long, spilling words upon meaningless words into every secret corner of his being.

Open Evening at the school was the next day, and Jack looked forward to an evening of quiet, alone in the house. Sheila always enjoyed this showcasing of the school's merits, and prepared diligently for it. She revelled in her organisational skills and the recognition of them from her colleagues, but most of all, she drank in the deference to her superiority that she knew was her right. She dressed to perfection usually, leaving nothing to chance, but this time, Jack realised she was taking a long time to get ready. He was about to hide himself away in the study, when she burst into the room behind him. Grabbing him by the arm, her fingers digging into his flesh, she hissed angrily at him, "You've got to help me, you useless lump!" Indicating her open mouth, she groaned, "I've got a dreadful toothache, you'll have to fix it, I can't go like this!"

Grabbing keys, she bundled him into the car, knowing as she drove to the surgery that it would be too late to catch Dennis, the locum, before he went home. Hastily, she opened the door and chivvied Jack in. With surprise, he saw that she was shaking, and he realised that she was actually in considerable pain, pain which, however, did nothing to stem the stream of words with which she was drowning him. She seated herself regally in the chair, and ordered him to begin. Jack gazed helplessly around, before slowly starting to gather the instruments he would need. A great crescendo of words swelled up from the depths of his brain, pushing, bruising, deafening, and he found himself repeating over and over in his mind, "Buy one, get one free!", "Take two, they're small", "Like the clappers! Like the clappers! Like the clappers!"

"Oh for God's sake" she screamed, "Stop making such a meal of it! You can't have forgotten this, as well as how to talk!" Throwing her head back dramatically, she said, "It's on the left, bottom row", before opening her large mouth as wide as she possibly could. Jack dithered for a moment, trying to make sense of the tangle of thoughts in his head. He couldn't think at all, distress overwhelming him as Sheila glared at him, her mouth still open.

He looked into the red maw of her throat, and saw, deep down, what was the trouble. Pouring from her purple-red throat, dark cavern, hell's gate, he heard all the shrieking, demonic, black words of the world come screaming, streaming, without end. He saw the great writhing clapper of her tongue, sending wave upon wave out to torment him.

"Pick it up and run with it! Pick it up…." sounded in the echoing cathedral of his body, reverberating through him like the rolling of majestic thunder. Calmly, in the quiet eye of the storm at last, he picked up a small sharp knife. Turning again to the abyss, he grasped her tongue firmly, shouting gaily "Open wide!" as he cut quickly and confidently into its muscular tenderness.

BETTY/ELIZABETH

"If I can just pick this thread through the back- oh, shit! It's torn!" Betty's eager fingers relaxed, and she held up the ripped garment. She had just spent almost an hour in a fruitless effort to rescue it. The clothes waiting to be washed lay in a heap on the floor. The potatoes wallowed in a basin of cold muddy water, waiting to be divested of their skins, then boiled to a mush, for she was sure to overcook them. Betty did'nt notice that her home was less than perfectly tidy, she really didn't need to, for Walter would be sure to point it out, anyway. He always did. Betty often wondered how she had managed to survive until Walter married her – or was it Walter who constantly wondered?

Betty pulled the sewing basket halfway out of the cupboard, and stuffed the garment hastily in, along with the other unfinished pieces of cloth.

"Out of sight, out of mind" she thought, almost closing the cupboard door.

Turning away, she noticed pale rings on the polished surface of the table, evidence for Walter that she spent time drinking tea, doing nothing useful, while he worked his fingers to the –

"Oh, don't even go there" she sighed, and stepped towards the place under the sink where the polish was kept, hitting her knee sharply on the slightly opened – or almost closed – cupboard door.

"Shit."

She said it again.

Sidetracked.

"Elizabeth is easily distracted" appeared on her school reports.

"Must learn to concentrate" was the comment on her piano teacher's report.

Standing irresolutely for a moment, Betty forgot why she was leaving the room, and then remembered that she wasn't. She turned again, this time not seeing the marks on the table, but the potatoes in the sink. Without enthusiasm, she began to tip the murky water down the drain.

****

Walter drove slowly, methodically. Around him, traffic poured out of the city, people rushing home, beeping horns, revving engines with exasperation, escaping. City centre traffic didn't frustrate him. Crowded restaurants didn't upset him. Awkward clients didn't ruffle his feathers. He never got road rage.

But Betty drove him, well, to distraction.

When they were first married, Betty, nine years his junior, bowed to his superior judgement – on everything. Betty's friends were most unsuitable. They called her Elizabeth, or Liz. He soon discouraged that. He took on the self-appointed task of moulding her, altering her, shaping her. He was skilled at altering, wearing down. He allowed little to please him, and she tried even harder. With a word or a look, a pursing of the lips, he had control. Whip hand. Oh yes, he had that all right.

But something wasn't right. After six years of marriage, Walter was not satisfied. Betty had changed. Far from being the pliable young bride he had taken, Betty no longer deferred to him as she once had. Her former eagerness to discuss, to ask, to comply, had begun to diminish. She had even Made Decisions without him – more than once. He had acted swiftly to discourage this, but it seemed that a worm of defiance had lodged in her, and the latest incident had left him somewhat shaken. Betty had retaliated, and had indulged in a most unseemly tussle, attempting to pull the belt from him. He had been obliged to punish her even more severely than he intended. In fact, she had not spoken to him since.

****

Betty/Elizabeth finished peeling the potatoes and put them in a saucepan of cold water. What to have with them? Mince? Fish? She giggled. Fish, for a cold fish. Pouring a glass of pineapple juice, she perched on the edge of a stool, hunching her shoulders, hands gripping the glass a little too tightly.

Betty/Elizabeth had been thinking a lot lately. Walter had thought for them both, but lately her own thoughts had begun to squeeze and slither out, whispering at first, now grumbling in ever more strident tones. It had a painful effect on her eyes. It forced them to open.

"How did it get to this?" she wondered. In the beginning, she was sure it was her fault. It was always Her Fault. Six years of being Her Fault. Last week was definitely Her Fault, although she would rather blame the pineapple juice.

They never bought pineapple juice, Walter didn't like it. But that afternoon, in the supermarket, in gesture of rebellion, she had reached quickly for the bright yellow carton before she had time to think. That evening, as Walter checked through the groceries as he always did, ticking them off against the receipt, he reeled in horror when he reached the unsanctioned purchase. Retribution was swift, but it didn't go as it often did, with Betty begging to be spared, and Walter magnanimously staying his hand after just a few strikes. Instead, Betty Elizabeth had screamed and bit and scratched and struggled, forcing him to retreat, disbelief mingled with rage on his face.

Betty/Elizabeth had hidden the pineapple juice. Now, it tasted sweet and smooth on her tongue. It tasted like forbidden fruit, laced with victory.

****

At the first set of traffic lights past the ring road, Walter allowed himself a moment of reflection, dwelling on his increasing difficulties with Betty. He would have to take a much stronger line – ultimately, perhaps, as drastic an action as he had taken with his first wife. Such a tragic accident. The police were perfectly satisfied.

The engine idled, and Walter flicked on the radio. Swelling music poured forth, and in time to the music he tapped the steering wheel, at the same time listing out loud the shortcomings of his wife. As the music reached a cresendo, he thumped Betty – no – the wheel harder, bellowing his displeasure.

"I deserve better, not Betty!" he thundered, his fists crashing down on the dashboard.

Suddenly aware of the cars waiting alongside, he glanced to his left. Looking directly at him, an amused smile playing about her lips, a sleekly groomed brunette nodded briefly in his direction. Walter stammered a weak smile, and gesticulated towards the dashboard, hoping she would presume that he had been transported by something uplifting and classical.

The lights changed, and she drew away, leaving Walter to fumble with the gears as he stalled the engine. Walter seldom daydreamed, but as he drove on at his usual stately pace, he permitted himself to speculate just a little. A cool elegant wife, a perfectly ordered home, novelle cuisine, impressed colleagues...control.

****

She suddenly moved off the stool. Leaving the glass unwashed, she walked into the hallway and gazed for a long time at the door, picturing him coming home as usual, his eyes darting around for possible punishable offences. She never knew what those might be – what passed his scrutiny one day might not the next. He would never be pleased. The fear that she had been suppressing rose like bile in her throat – she rushed to the bathroom and was painfully sick. Afterwards, she accepted what she knew she must do, and walked heavily and mechanically upstairs.

Opening the wardrobe, she considered what she should take. The clothes, chosen by him, making her older, made her someone else. Pulling them from their hangers, she flung them around the room, ripping and tearing. Tears of anger at herself stung her cheeks.

Hysterical, she toppled furniture, spilt shampoo and aftershave, scattered talcum powder. Then, trembling with reverberating stress, she stopped. Calmly, she walked downstairs, not at all distracted. Going to his desk, she found the key he had fancied she was too stupid to discover. He always closed the study door while he counted out the grocery money he gave her, so she knew it was in there somewhere.

Glancing at her watch, Elizabeth/Betty knew she must hurry. Just minutes later, she found it.

Quickly grabbing as much as she could cram into her shoulder bag, she stumbled from the room, a trail of notes fluttering along behind her. Into the kitchen, she lifted the carton of pineapple juice, then walked deliberately upstairs again, her heart becoming lighter at every step.

She hummed a little as she heaped his expensive suits on the bed, then slowly and pleasurably drizzled the rest of the pineapple juice over them.

Leaving the door swinging gently open, Elizabeth left.

****

The last traffic lights before turning off the main road were just ahead when Walter noticed the brunette again. His heart gave a little pleasing skip, and he decided to draw level, perhaps catch her eye again. She was a little ahead, so he accelerated rather more quickly than he intended. Witnesses agreed there was nothing the driver of the oil tanker could have done to avoid him.

Walter was easily distracted.

RACY, LACY

"The last time I saw Hugo", said Moira conversationally, "was at my wedding, and at the time, I was completely naked, so I suppose he's a little embarrassed."

We had watched Hugo dodge the traffic to cross the busy road – it had seemed to me that he was avoiding us. I stood still for a moment, taking in what she had so casually said, and she smiled at my astonished expression, saying,

"I'm well aware that some of my friends are quite uncomfortable when in my company now, but I really don't care. Oh, I forgot you were away at the time. Have you really not heard about my wedding? No? Well, I don't know how you missed it – it was unforgettable. Have you time for a coffee? I must tell you all about it – don't worry, I won't cry or make a scene! "

We took our seats in a nearby cafe, and Moira began.

"I remember sitting on the edge of my bed that morning, trying to hold onto my wedding dress, but the glossy material spilled through my fingers, it's glistening folds cascading in a sibilant rush to the floor. Maybe it was a sign of some sort, but if it was, I chose to ignore it. I was wearing deep crimson, sexy underwear, not my usual choice, but Alan had bought it, so I wore it anyway. It was lavishly trimmed with layers of lace, which scratched a little, and I wriggled uncomfortably.

My wedding day, at last.

I had planned a quiet wedding, but somehow it mushroomed alarmingly, as weddings often do. It seemed that every friend and relative we had were even now assembling at the church where, in less than an hour, I would arrive, the cynosure of all eyes. I shivered at the thought. My twin sister, Jennifer, on the other hand, had relished being the centre of attention at her own wedding almost a year ago to Neil, and seemed to be re-living it all over again in organising me. Through the thin walls of my flat, I could clearly hear Jennifer's voice raised in argument with the hairdresser, while calling to the kitchen for tea, and berating the other hapless bridesmaids. Jennifer was in her element.

I wondered how loud Jennifer would be if she realised that I had discovered a secret, just this morning. I fingered the lace idly. What should I do?

In the small sitting room, our Mother sat quietly, keeping out of the way. She had the beginning of a headache, and I'm sure we both wished that Jennifer would lower her voice.

It was time to put on my dress, to feel that silky fabric slide over my head and down my body to the floor. Time to wear the sparkly high heels, the demure veil, and the fine silver necklace that Alan had sent to his "darling bride". Not the red sexy bra with the scratchy lace, and the barely-there knickers, meant for someone else, but delivered to me by mistake.

I was hurt and heartbroken, anyone would be, and also angry and confused, I had no idea what to do. My eyes were dry and burning, my throat seemed to be closed and I was hardly able to breathe.

Then there was a rap at the door, and I heard whispering and muffled laughter.

"Moira! Are you decent? Can we come in?"

It was three of my closest friends, so I quickly pulled on a dressing gown to hide the red underwear, and opened the door. They burst into the room, falling in a giggling heap on my bed.

"God, Moira, you're not even dressed yet!"

"Oh look – your beautiful dress is on the floor – for heaven's sake!"

"We were trying to get past Jennifer before she saw us, she's relentless, isn't she?"

So there I was, trying to stay coherent and functioning, while they fussed and chattered around me. I had to let them dress me, though I had a job explaining away the red underwear. I just knew if I let myself go, I'd never stop crying. At last, I closed the door behind them, and then I locked it. I needed a few minutes to think. Jennifer banged and rattled at the door a few times, but I ignored her.

What should I do?

I gazed into the mirror, mesmerised by my shining reflection. The dress was more than beautiful, it was magical. It shimmered as I twisted from side to side, a perfect fit. Jennifer had bullied me into buying it – I had thought it was too sophisticated for me – but she was right. She certainly had good taste. The little veil, embroidered with tiny crimson rosebuds was just right, perfectly matching the deep crimson of the bridesmaid's dresses. Yes, great sense of style, our Jennifer.

The shoes were the only thing I picked myself – we had an argument in the shop I remember. Jennifer wanted me to get dainty crimson shoes, but I fell in love with a pair of spiky, sparkly, high, high heels. Then, in the middle of our dispute, her phone rang. She glanced at the screen, then rushed outside to take the call, her face flushed. While she was outside, I bought the shoes I wanted, though I expected her to try to change them, but she just muttered something about an "appointment" and rushed away.

Yes, the shoes were the only thing I picked myself.

"Moira! The taxis are here!" Jennifer bellowed, "Let's get this show on the road!"

I watched as the bridesmaids and the tiny flower girl tumbled into the taxi – Jennifer rolled down the window and yelled at me to hurry. Mum was giving me away, I suppose you know my father left us years ago to live with a woman younger than me, in California. Weird, isn't it?

I really wanted to tell Mum everything, to ask her what I should do, but instead I just hugged her tightly and we got into the taxi.

"At last, the show's on the road" she said happily, and I felt so guilty, because there could be no show. No ceremony, no vows.

No exchanging a glance that acknowledged all our sweet secrets in one intimate moment.

Our secrets.

His secret.

I was in a daze, only seeing the note that had fallen out of the box of red sexy underwear. Only think about the explicit message in Alan's handwriting with someone else's name on it. The taxi pulled up at the church, and I still didn't know what to do. There was a flurry of bridesmaids, hands pulling at my dress, fixing my hair, then Mum took my arm and said" Ready?"

No, I wasn't ready, but I nodded and together we walked up the aisle. When we got to where Alan stood waiting, I was almost suffocating, couldn't speak nor breathe.

What should I do?

The minister was talking, but nothing made sense to me, then out of the confusion in my head, I distinctly heard the words 'know of any just cause' and I shouted out. It was just a jumble of words, but I had to stop him somehow. His mouth opened with surprise, and a low murmur rippled through the congregation.

Nervously, he asked again, "If anyone knows of – "but before he finished I shouted out clearly,

"I do!"

Jennifer went pale, I thought she was going to faint as she looked over at Neil, her husband, panic-stricken. Alan turned away from me, the back of his neck flushed a dull, guilty red. Neither of them spoke.

Then I went a bit crazy, I think.

"This dress was bought for me" I shrieked, then I hitched it up to reveal the red sexy knickers, and I yelled "But these weren't!"

I wrenched the dress off over my head and threw it at Jennifer, still shouting.

"You picked it – you keep it!"

I started to turn away, then stopped. I peeled off the bra first, then I stepped out of the red sexy knickers, and flung them in Jennifer's face.

"You might as well have these too, you'll probably need them later, if his note is anything to go by!"

Then I walked down the aisle, wearing the only thing I'd picked myself – the spiky, sparkly, high, high heels.

Hugo, bless him, stepped out into the aisle and tried to put his jacket around me, but I shrugged it off without stopping. It's all a bit hazy after that."

Moira leaned back in her chair, folding her arms, looking intently at me for my reaction.

"Well, that's the story of my wedding," she said.

I was speechless. She leaned forward again, and asked,

"So, what would you have done?"

"I just can't imagine" I replied, and there was a short strained silence for a couple of minutes, then awkwardly, stupidly, I asked,

"Did your sister ever apologise? Did you manage to make it up with her?"

"What? Make up?" Moira snapped. "Of course not! Could you? Anyway, they disappeared soon after that, they haven't been heard of since – I don't suppose they ever will."

We paid for our coffee, and stood for a moment, saying the usual things – 'lovely to see you, we must do it again,' and so on. Then Moira said brightly,

"Do you know, I still don't remember how I got home that day? It can't have been on the bus, anyway!' she laughed.

And she walked away, wriggling her shoulder a little as she went, adjusting an uncomfortable bra strap – a faded, red sexy strap with tattered red lace.

LOCO THOUGHTS FROM THE MESETA

FOR ONE NIGHT ONLY

I was famous in Hornillos
For one night only.
The hospitalero gave a great shout of recognition
When he saw my camino painting on my camera.
'That's my camino!' he shouted,
then he ran up the street to call his friend
to come and see
me.
People crowded into the house,
Queuing to have their photo taken
With a famous irish artist
And a quiet japanese girl placed an order.
They passed my camera from hand to hand,
Flicking through the images,
The batteries running down as they all
Had a peep.
A party started.
It was mad, all mad.

SANCHO PANZA

Clowns in and out of my days
And I a clown in theirs,
In a blur of blended voices, colours, yellow dust.
Meseta.
Wide, wide skies.
Tilting at windmills on the roof of the world
With a crazy woman from Logrono,
Flying on the wind with outstretched arms,
Screaming like children,

The wind turbines waving slowly, elegantly
Above Sancho Panza from Logrono-
Did she really have sex with Jose in the undergrowth?-
I didn't wait to find out.
A car came sailing into the air
And landed sideways in a stubble field-
The driver ran around the field,
Stumbling and reeling as though he were drunk,
Maybe he was.
It was the most normal thing that happened
That day.

I HAD A SHOWER

Sitting in the sun.
Checked in early,
Had a shower.
I'm in first, got the best bed.
Smug.
It's only twelve thirty.
All day, pilgrims come-
And go.
Not smug now, six thirty-five
And there's nobody in this hostal
except me.
Surely I don't smell?
I've had a shower!.
(these are the boring bits we don't talk about!)

LIGHTS OUT

They said,
"Come and eat with us at our hostal-
come at seven."
So I came.
Hungry.
"Ah Pauline! You come! Now we go to buy

something to eat-
You can buy the tomatoes, and the bread and the..''
'Yes' I say quickly,
and so we go.
To a bar.
We talk, we drink, we talk, we talk.
It's 8.05pm, I'm hungry.
At last, we go to the shop, we buy.
Back at their hostal, there's a queue for the cooker.
So we talk, we drink, we talk some more.
It's 8.45pm, I starving.
Finally, we cook, we eat.
It's 9.50pm.
My hostal is one kilometre away.
Lights go out at 10.pm.

BUTLINS

I couldn't get on the train,
The step was too high, so
They called for help.
Help wore a bright yellow jacket
Trimmed liberally with red and gold.
He took my arm and walked proudly,
Stately, as though I were a princess.
I felt conspicuous.
At Burgos, he escorted me to the taxi, courteously, gently.
I felt proud.

SERAPHIN

At the edge of the village, pilgrims gather at the fountain,
Feet burning, ankles aching from the stony ground,
the heat, the hornets buzzing spitefully.
Ten kilometres in the fierce sun, no shade.
When will the albergue open?

Suddenly, the door flies open and a crazy-looking guy hurtles out,
Stumbles, almost at my feet,
Recovers himself, stands up straight,
Replaces his hat
And yells at me
"What do you want?"
"A bed" I say, and he nods,
but says sharply,
"I am cleaning, you wait one hour. One hour you wait".
I sit on a stone wall and say,
"I wait".

About 20 other pilgrims crowd to the door,
But he pushes them away, screaming,
"Go away! You can't come in! This is not the albergue
with the Olympic swimming pool!
Go away!"
A norwegian woman manages to squeeze past
And tries to advance up the path leading to a hidden garden,
But he shoves her out, yelling,
"This is not the albergue with the Olympic swimming pool!
You only want to look because you want the best – you are not a real pilgrim!
Go away! You can't come in!" He lunges at the other pilgrims,
Swinging his stick wildly, and they move hastily away.
I sit on the wall, waiting.
He grabs my arm and pulls me through the door,
Closing it with a crash behind us.

We enter the garden of eden.
Fig trees, apples, pears, lemons,
Grapes, all heavy with fruit.
Against the white-painted walls, flowers
Mixed with peppers, courgettes, tomatoes
Beans, oh a whole cornucopia of fresh, fresh foods.
Trees sway gently in the hot breath of the meseta,
A hammock, some chairs and tables,

Green lawns, well tended, and.......
A swimming pool.
Not Olympic sized, but bigger than the one at the other side of the village.
Nice irony.
"What is your name?"
I tell him.
"Oh!" he says. "I will call you Mac!"
As the afternoon wears on, he screams abuse at the pilgrims rattling the door.
Just once, he asks a few questions, then drags a young Canadian girl in,
Pours us a beer.
Seraphin in his garden, smoking, talking through the fragrance,
More beer.
More smoke.
"Mac, you are the queen of this albergue, tonight you do nothing.
Just relax. We will cook...Riley from Canada, can you cook?"
About two hours later, a very burnt, inedible omlette appears,
There is nothing else.
There is no shop in this village.....and anyway.......
I'm sooooooo relaxed!
Canada, Ireland and Spain
Playing dominoes.
We talk nonsense all evening, Seraphin says,
"a pilgrim must have humility, patience and adaptation"
I say, the camino gives so much...some for your life, some for sharing,
and some for letting go'
we imagine we are profound.
Goodnight.

SO HOT

Did I pray?
Or just beg for a bed?
Hot. So hot.
And the butterflies!
Oh! the colours!
The yellow dust,

The pale mountains in the distance.
Day's end, thinking of beds.
Yurts, log cabins, cold concrete,
Teepees, put up carelessly-
No, I didn't sleep there.
Bunks, bumping my head,
Thinking of Aileen's scones in the morning
When there is no breakfast.

AS IF IT MATTERS

'What time do you leave in the morning?'
As if it matters.
They're going to wake you up anyway,
Sifting through their plastic bags,
Sudden swift flashes of torchlight,
Heavy boots dropping on the floor,
Coughing, farting, spitting,
And their self control breaks at last
so they turn on the light
At 5.35am.
'What time do you leave in the morning?'
Whenever.